The Dangerous Age

Also by Annette Williams Jaffee

Adult Education
Recent History

The Dangerous Age

A Novel

Annette Williams Jaffee

Leapfrog Press
Wellfleet, Massachusetts

Published in 1999 in the United States by
The Leapfrog Press
P. O. Box 1495
Wellfleet, MA 02667-1495
www.leapfrogpress.com

Distributed in the United States by
Consortium Book Sales and Distribution
St. Paul, Minnesota 55114

First Edition

Library of Congress Cataloging-in-Publication Data

Jaffee, Annette Williams, 1945–
    The dangerous age : a novel / by Annette Williams Jaffee. – 1st ed.
       p. cm.
    ISBN 0-9654578-4-2
    I. Title
    PS3560.A317D36 1999   98-17253
    813´.54–DC21   CIP

10 9 8 7 6 5 4 3 2

Printed in the United States of America

This is for John

Acknowledgments

I would like to thank the Corporation of Yaddo for time spent there, which yielded an early draft of this novel.

Suzanne's theories about fairy tales and the lives of the saints were gleaned from Marina Warner's remarkable book, *From the Beast to the Blonde*.

And many thanks to M., who remains my fairy godmother.

A *grande passion* is as rare as a masterpiece.
—Balzac

PART I

1

A bedroom in Paris, everything white: sheets, walls, a long ceramic dish of narcissus, the reflection of the moon on the river outside the windows, a medieval wall bleached by moonlight, a scented candle flickering on the mantel.

She sits and faces him, this man, almost a stranger. She sits on his bare thick thighs, straddling his thighs. She feels his large strong hands divide her back with its bony trail, reach for places hidden from her; her face is in the crook of his shoulder, her mouth on his neck, her hands on the sides of his face. His scent is new, but familiar: citrus, vetiver. She will devour him, she will save him, she will worship him for giving this back to her.

A bedroom near Chicago; her husband's voice, abrupt, impatient: "Suzanne. . . ?"

"Hm. . . ?"

"Are you finished?"

"What?"

"Did you come?"

"Oh, yes . . . yes, yes."

"Good."

Suzanne felt him roll off, watched as he padded away. She touched her cheek, it was wet, she was crying. She was thinking about a man she had loved when she was twenty. "Alain," she said when she heard the water pounding from the shower.

She grabbed her robe, her slippers, shuffled downstairs, flicked on the coffee maker. She reached for the dog's leash. In the window's reflection, she saw a small woman with a mass of fading reddish hair. The old dog yawned and they stepped outside together, blurry eyed, to fetch the paper from the end of the long frosty driveway. Commuters on their early way into the city passed, someone appeared to recognize her, raised a tentative, gloved hand, she turned too late to respond.

"The Volvo needs to be brought in this morning," Barry was saying. "Don't forget to tell them about the windshield wipers, this time." He unfolded the paper and pushed the Home section across the table to her place. "Can you get a ride from someone in your office? I have a late appointment. Where did you put that jam I brought back from California?"

She rose, found it immediately. It was in front of the milk on the top shelf of the refrigerator.

"God, this stuff is great. You can't find anything

like this here."

They had recently returned from the Napa Valley where they had celebrated their twenty-fifth wedding anniversary in a small luxurious hotel stuck precariously on a hill above the vineyards. That morning they had taken a hot air balloon ride over the area and Barry had toasted their clever good fortune as they drank local champagne in a field of wild poppies. That night, after a heart-stopping dinner of sautéed *foie gras* and chanterelles, veal chops tied with sage and fig tarts with armagnac *gelato*, Barry had made love to her. (Twice a week: a sex life based on some national statistic.) Afterward, Suzanne had gone into the Italian tiled bathroom and turned the shower on full blast and wept because she knew she would have to sleep with this man for the rest of her life. He would certainly outlive her.

February: a day that begins in darkness with a lecture on women and myth. This was Women's Studies, a study of everything that came before, but from a woman's perspective.

"Imagine Pocahontas," she told her class. "She is 13. Maybe she has been off collecting berries—they say we were gatherers. Or perhaps she is in the teepee of her aunt weaving baskets with the women when she hears them bringing in the

15

prisoner. Maybe she was sent there by her father so she will not witness what happens next. She is 13, she is motherless."

Suzanne flicked a slide onto the screen behind her: a pastel-washed drawing from a children's book. Pocahontas' round girlish arms encircle the bearded head of Captain John Smith resting awkwardly on the block as warriors surround him with raised axes. If she were teaching about myth and men, she might mention the historically incorrect method of execution and that white-haired John Smith was only 32 at the time.

"Does she cry to the mighty and great Powhatan, 'Save him, father, I want him for my own?' Like some of our Biblical ancestors, Pocahontas seems to have a predilection for strangers, a fascination with the unfamiliar: scent, taste, language, custom. She apparently loves their unpredictability, the inability to place them, to know their lives.

Not long after this, she was abducted by the colonists and held hostage in the complicated inevitability of those early skirmishes. But before she is returned to her people, she has fallen in love with another John, John Rolfe. She marries him and goes with him to England to live."

Suzanne clicked, pivoted, replaced the picture of the girl with an engraving of Pocahontas made shortly after her arrival in England.

"Here we see her at 22, as elegant as any lady of the court—where she was an enormous success, by the way. She is dressed *à la mode*, a smart bowler perches on her striking black hair; pearls drop from her tiny ears, a starched ruff surrounds her long thin neck. Pocahontas. Rebecca Rolfe. Imagine."

That was what Suzanne did, this was her trick. She was like Scheherezade, but with a twist. She was a fortune teller, but in reverse—she imagined for others. She recreated what had been lost, conjured up the objects and moments of the past. When she looked into their sleepy, dulled eyes and saw something recorded there—excitement or recognition or even a kind of educated dreaminess—she knew she had been a success.

The end of office hours: Suzanne saw the last of her students, ostensibly about a topic for her final paper, but the girl suddenly burst into tears. She is pressured, passionate. She doesn't know if she really wants to teach, but her parents think it is a good idea; she doesn't know if she wants to marry, but the young man who loves her thinks it is a good idea. Here she twisted the shiny ring on her finger—a beacon of brilliant light in the fluorescent office gloom.

"What should I do?" she begged.

From where Suzanne sat, she could see the cold flat lake and clusters of students and the trees stretching their skeletal limbs towards the dead gray sky. If she leaned a certain way she could see the magnificent doily dome of the Bha'i Temple, but she could not see the future.

She wished to say something comforting, or at least intelligent, supportive. In the past, she might have talked about all the possibilities of a woman's life, she might have even cited episodes from her own life; she would have compared it to weaving or knitting, called it a giant tapestry made from friends and children and work, but she found lately she couldn't say a thing. It was as if her throat was parched, dry with disease.

In her dreams she was always falling off the edge of things: cliffs, ladders, missing the final step to slip down a flight of stairs, or hanging from the severed limb of a great tree. Nothing seemed clear. She went back to the eye doctor again and again, until, finally, to get rid of her, he prescribed glasses, simple magnifying glasses she could have bought for a fraction of the cost at the local dime store.

Everything she had imagined was completed, her children were almost grown, away from home: Joshua was in law school, Amy was finishing her junior year of college. She lived in a large, handsome home furnished with objects and books and pieces of furniture that reflected a life time of travel and taste and interest. She had an old dog. A book based on the dissertation she had finally completed after almost twenty interrupted years of graduate study was being published later in the spring.

It was the best of times, it was the worst of times. Everyone who was going to divorce, had, and now they were starting to die. A woman with whom she had come to the college was dying of breast cancer; another had been recently diagnosed. A colleague who taught history was hospitalized with AIDS; one of her husband's friends suffered a heart attack on the tennis courts one Sunday morning. He was 51.

Even the children were not safe: a boy from her son's class in high school skidded his Honda Civic into a Vermont snow bank and was killed instantly. A neighbor's daughter, 26, pregnant with her first child, dropped dead suddenly of a clot to her brain on the streets of Seattle. Suzanne brushed off her black jersey dress and her black suede pumps and marched obediently to the college chapel and then she put them carefully away for what she knew would be more frequent appearances.

"Don't do it," she said to the student.

"What? Don't do what?" She jumped, seemed alarmed.

"Oh, dear, I don't know," Suzanne said and glanced at her watch. She shuffled some papers and began impatiently to pack her briefcase, the traditional signaling of the end of the conference. "Maybe the issues of personal freedom in *To The Lighthouse*," she said helpfully, although no one had mentioned the novel at all.

2

Suzanne met Robert in an exercise class during this long, wet winter. He was a banker with a bad back.

Robert Parrish left his office early. Heading north from the Loop before the traffic, he drove directly to a fitness center near the Northwestern campus. His orthopedist had recommended exercise for his bruised back, this low impact dance class with an emphasis on Stretch and Flex. He changed and stood in the back of the dark studio, alone, for thirty minutes sometimes, waiting patiently for his fellow students, women: housewives with older children, secretaries, teachers from the elementary school nearby.

Suzanne was frequently late, always in a hurry. That winter she wore a big rough coat her husband had discarded years ago, a field coat from a hunting catalog, outsized, the leather collar turned up, and long soft scarves and twice-wrapped mufflers she unwound and discarded as she hurried into the studio. When it rained or snowed, she wore a big felt hat that hid her face and made her look young and vulnerable.

Shunning the locker room, she undressed in the back where it was shadowy and there were hooks and benches, undressed the way dancers learn in tight studio situations, with a minimum of movement and a maximum of grace, stepping out of faded jeans, pulling up leotards under one of the big sweatshirts from their schools or teams her children had given her over the years.

There had been a narrow space like this at the first ballet school she had attended, an enclosed porch of the neighborhood house where Miss Morgan had founded her School of Dance. She remembered shivering out of her clothes—winter in Boston—and into her leotards as a child of five and six. The mothers sat on benches and knitted while the little girls took class. Sometimes, afterwards, they would go out for tea and tiny cakes with one of the other mothers.

She still wore ballet leotards with long sleeves and low necks and backs, footless tights pulled over the leotards and rolled at the waist for accent, everything black or pink, everything worn and stretched and a hundred years old. Dressed, she squatted and shook her big leather handbag until it revealed a covered elastic. Standing loosely, leaning on one hip, pressing her crooked feet into a high arch by pushing back on her toes, bending them under, she twisted her long wild hair into a careful chignon with several quick turns of her hands. She had been doing this all her life.

She knew Robert watched her. She wondered if he simply liked to observe women in those private moments Degas captured in his art. She had read somewhere that Degas was the first chronicler of working women: dancers, circus performers, laundresses, prostitutes.

Robert's interest in her at first was that simple, about gesture, movement. He had been an athlete as a young man, taken pleasure in the ability of his body to execute certain feats with grace and ease. He ran cross-country, he did the decathlon, he raced French bicycles across the low mountain ranges of his boyhood California under the sponsorship of a local shop. A football scholarship had propelled him from a small valley town to the university and his present life, and he admired her ability to perform the intricate steps, the careful placement of hands and feet. He had never attended the ballet in his life. Oh, once they took the children to the Nutcracker at Christmas.

She smiled at him sometimes, but she rarely spoke—this wasn't a social occasion for her. The banter, the gossip, the normal pleasantries were beneath her; she was serious, aloof. She knew the other women thought she was showing off, but she had stopped worrying about being popular after high school. She began to look forward to Robert's attention; she found herself playing to it sometimes, becoming more balletic, dreamier and yet making the movements sharper, more precise, the way she had learned.

As for him, he was so drawn to her, to her movements that were so graceful, intensely female, they seemed almost holy. He stood as close to her as he felt proper, watching the small sharp turning of her head, the sweep of her arched arms, the quick light movements of her feet. He sensed a connection between the two of them, as if they alone understood this life of the body, its integrity and the beauty of bone, muscle, flesh.

Once, she came early so she could tape her left ankle. She had tripped on the dog's lead that morning, but refused to miss a class. She sat with one leg tucked under, distracted, intense, twisting the flesh colored elastic bandages in a careful figure eight. Raising her head, she looked up and saw Robert watching and asked, "Do you go in for bondage?"

He laughed in surprise. "I was thinking about football. They used to shave our legs to here." He bent and tapped his shin. "Before they taped them. Otherwise you'd pull the hair off, too. The pain would be terrible."

She winced, and in a voice so low he had to lean very close to hear, described how she was taught to fashion a small slipper of gauze to tuck inside a toe shoe; how the blisters never hardened enough to callous, because the next day you opened them again, and how the lambswool she stuffed into the toes would become so encrusted with blood she had to soak it to loosen.

"See, smooth," he said, indicating his shin.

She ran her hand across it.

"The hair never grows back."

3

In May, her book was published. Based on her dissertation, it connected the lives of the saints to the earliest fairy tales, those of Basile and Perrault. Her academic training was in art history; she was an expert in the Early Renaissance depiction of female martyrs: Catherine's spiky wheel, Barbara and her burning tower, Lucy holding her eyes like branched cherries, Agatha offering her own breasts like bon-bons on a platter—hearts and bones.

She used the lives of these early saints and their counterparts in fairy tales—*Cinderella* and *Snow White* and *The Maid with Wooden Hands*—as metaphors for contemporary women's lives, the abuse and incest, the fragile attempts to escape the demands and advances of powerful men: fathers and husbands and brothers.

Remarkably, the book, published by an arcane university press, was noticed by a researcher at *TIME* and featured in a cover piece on women and the church. There was something slightly awkward about being presented in a collage that included Mother Theresa, Joan of Arc, Madonna and some militant nuns from Detroit. Amy left an excited message that she had bought out every copy at the school store and the local 7-Elevens. Josh's old college girl friend called to say she had seen it in Hong Kong. Barry seemed beside himself with pleasure. He sent copies of it to people he knew, with his card, he pushed her to call her publisher and make demands. He always knew she had it in her, he said.

Robert told Suzanne he saw it while waiting to get a haircut near his office.

"I guess it's my fifteen minutes."

"I'm sorry?" he said.

"Andy Warhol. He said everyone in America would be famous for fifteen minutes."

"Oh," Robert said.

"I suppose you don't think much about Andy Warhol."

"I know who he was," he replied seriously.

"He also said that the truly brave people are stepmothers and baby sitters. And maybe brides. Colette wrote that of all forms of courage, that of girls must be the greatest or there would be fewer marriages."

He looked confused.

She knew she was lecturing, for a change. "I have a feeling your Sixties and mine were not the

28

same."

"Oh, you were one of those crazy hippies waving banners." He shook his fists above his head. "I was working on Wall Street then and I would see you all the time."

"Handing out flowers? No, that wasn't me. Anyway, all you white men in blue suits looked the same to me."

"Is that how you view me? A white man in blue suit?" He looked down at his knit shirt and jogging shorts.

"Absolutely. I would say you are the archetypical white man in a blue suit."

"You might be surprised," he said. "About me." He ran his hands over his thick hair. "I had a pretty rough youth in the Valley."

"The Valley?"

"The San Joaquin Valley. *The Grapes of Wrath*."

"Chavez," she said. "I helped organize the grape boycott on the North Shore. I suppose you didn't participate in that?"

He laughed and shook his head. "I'm from Bakersfield."

"Bakersfield," she said. "That's a mythic American place. We're supposed to spend a leave at Berkeley next year."

"I played football for Cal in the early Fifties. I think you'll like it there," he said.

She doubted it, she didn't want go anywhere, but she nodded politely and took her usual place in the front.

A flurry of local publicity accompanied the publication of her book. Suzanne was photographed in her study, surrounded by reproductions of paintings of her favorite saints, on the wide porch of her house, and walking along the Lake with her old greyhound, Lucia, whom she had acquired many years before from an organization that saved these dogs from early death. Lucia's sins had been loyalty and a torn ankle. She remembered when she picked her up at the kennel. She was only two years old and her leg had been badly set; she was skinny and shivering from pain and fear, as if she knew what she had escaped. Suzanne remembered her looking through those fine brown eyes with rare knowledge and gratitude, love. Sometimes the dog's love for her was almost too much to bear. It made her feel guilty; she couldn't live up to it. She thought it must be like the love of saints, a love pure and clean and free of doubt. So she named her Lucia, whom the Romans had martyred by plucking out her eyes. It took months for her to come when called. Bea's Ransom had been her name at the track.

She remembered the first time she had seen Lucia run. After the ankle had healed, Suzanne had taken her for a walk along the lake and let her off the lead. Lucia suddenly spotted a squirrel and took off as if the sadistic invincible rabbit was ahead of her. Suzanne would never forget the way her body almost folded in half like an antique foundry bellows and then exploded into powerful leaps, her slender proud head high, her long legs taking wide graceful strides and magnificent jetés.

Suzanne's life in the ballet had ended with an embolism in her left leg when she was fifteen. She had danced on it and danced on it until it bloomed into a clot that finally sent a dizzy red line up her leg on its way to her heart. She fainted on the MTA, *pointe* shoes in her bag, and was rushed to Mass. General for surgery and a month on her back. It occurred soon after her mother's death and she connected the two events: her mother would have noticed, her mother would have cared, she would not have allowed it to happen. This was punishment for being adolescent and self-absorbed, being callous and careless; maybe, she just wanted to die, too. Ballet had been her mother's gift, it was their secret language, their connection at the worst times; the double loss signaled the end of childhood with one flip of a master switch.

She did not tell the reporters about the ballet, she just talked about the dog. "How would you like to be put to death because your so-called usefulness is finished?" she would ask with indignation.

She talked about her children, too. Josh, her first born, was at the University of Michigan Law School, interested in first amendment issues. Amy, a politics major at Oberlin, would be spending the summer teaching at a primary school in Haiti. She outlined Barry's career from a clerkship for Justice Douglas to his professorship at Northwestern Law School. She divulged her recipe for zucchini bread.

When pressed she told them she was working on another book, a history of housewives in nineteenth century literature. Hedda and Nora, Emma B. and Anna K.: bad girls, bored girls, a whole literature dreamed up by men about wayward wives and mothers. She was planning to call it *The Last Housewife*, which was how she thought of herself as she served the zucchini bread and freshly brewed coffee and tea. The local reporters sometimes forgot the book, but always mentioned the baked goods, and the large house, her husband's prominence, her children's academic success. It made her wince; it made her fearful. She thought of her mother's grandmother's admonitions to tie a red ribbon around the wrists of her children or to toss salt over her shoulder or to spit into the wind. She wanted to open her messy closets or expose her stony marriage or confide her children's personal problems to ward off the evil eye.

She gave a talk at the local library that Robert attended. She opened, as she usually did, with the story of *The Donkeyskin*.

"It's the story of a king who promises his dying wife that he will marry again, but only to a woman with hair of gold and as beautiful as she. After years of searching far and wide, gathering princesses from the ends of the earth, he realizes their adolescent daughter is the only one who fits the job description and announces their wedding will take place the following day. So here we have the oldest fairy tale we know, and it deals with sexual abuse," she said.

"The daughter, who is probably about fifteen, is terrified, of course, and consults an old woman in the forest who tells her to cover herself with the skin of an ass when her father comes to her bed that night. As she predicted, he is so repelled, it gives her a chance to escape."

She told other stories: maidens who cut off their hands or hid in barrels to get away from angry or amorous fathers and husbands. "There was even a

saint who grew a beard on her wedding day and
her husband had her beheaded." She flashed a slide
of a Northern Renaissance altarpiece on a screen
behind her of a young female face with a straggly
triangular beard flowing from her pretty chin. "For
centuries she was the patron saint of wives." She
waited professionally for the laughter.

Smoothly she connected the life of St.
Catherine to Snow White's.

"When the soldiers refused to kill Catherine
of Alexandria, her father had them all killed—
two hundred of them—and then he hired more.
And when the wicked Queen instructs the hunter
to bring back proof of Snow White's death, he
brings the heart of a boar because he cannot bear
to kill the beautiful princess. I guess this proves
that hunters and soldiers are kinder than parents,"
she said.

The audience laughed again, but Robert
cringed. He had three daughters and he had been
a soldier in a war fought on foreign soil against
men whose daughters he shared. He remembered
taking home a girl for a night of sex and making
love to her behind a flimsy paper screen while
her family slept or listened. In the morning he
paid her father in canned goods and cigarettes.
He wanted to tell Suzanne that she was wrong
and she was right, but not for the reasons she

thought. He wondered how she could make pro-
nouncements about things she did not know. He
didn't say a thing, of course, he just shook her
hand afterward, during the cookies and punch. She
was surprised to see him there.

He was reading her book in the evenings alone
in the library of his house on the Lake. He found
it obtuse and pedantic. It referred to events in history, and paintings and documents he didn't know
or remember. His knowledge of fairy tales was
dim, too. He seemed to know only the pretty
Disney versions.

This had become the pattern of his life since
his youngest daughter had been sent to boarding
school that year: work, the exercise class three
times a week. Usually his wife Louise joined him
for dinner on a tray in front of the TV news.
Then, while she made phone calls and did her
committee things, he read alone until bedtime.
At 10:30 he made the coffee and set the timer for
6:35 AM. He gave his wife a peck on the cheek
and retired to the bedroom where he had slept
alone for seven years.

There were reasons for it, of course: his snoring, his insomnia, his leg cramps, Louise's extreme
sensitivity to noise and light. He had started by
simply finding an empty bedroom (as the girls

grew, there seemed to be plenty of them). When the first daughter married, he moved into her room officially; a decorator was hired to change the chintz to stripes. Louise had studied *faux* with this famous man who could date furniture by tasting the glue.

Robert thought Suzanne's book was probably clever, but there was a basic sadness to her premise, a cynicism about men. He wondered if it was her own experience, her own life she was drawing on. He thought of her remark about the courage of brides. Every few pages, he found himself flipping to the rather stark photograph of her on the back. He discovered that, amazingly, she had been born in a small town in Texas where his mother's people came from and he began to think about those boyhood summers with a deep pleasure he had not felt for a long time. He couldn't fit this one fact, geographical, into the urban, intellectual life that was outlined on the jacket flap. It, Texas, reached out like a streaking comet to him, and made him feel strangely close to her.

Later, when he asked her about it, she said this must have been the reason her father had been stationed there for six months at the end of the war, so she could be born in an army hospital on a freezing Texas morning, for this, for him, so they could make this connection.

4

Suzanne and Barry spent the next year in Berkeley. Suzanne realized immediately that it would be a replay of the early years of their marriage: it was Barry's choice, his position, his reasons for being there; she was alone, childless.

She had married at 21, gratefully, not entirely capriciously. She had known him all her life—their families were friendly, their paternal grandfathers were distant relations in that other, old world. Suzanne's was a classic tale: a dead mother, a frantic grieved father, a silly stepmother with two small children and needs of her own. In a fairy tale, she would have been sent out to forage her way with a heel of bread, outwitting birds and witches and monsters along the way until she met the Prince. Instead, it was a matter of finding a good school until that happened.

A hazy first memory of Barry—or had his mother told her this?—she was four, he was an important nine and they were playing hide and go seek at a cousin's club picnic in a forest preserve.

He hid far from the grown-ups in an arcade of deep cover. She wandered gamely out, calling his name, frightened by the thick trees and darkness and silence, and when she got close to where he was hiding, he jumped out of the bushes and grabbed her. He scared her so much, she wet her pants. She remembered the dress she was wearing: white seersucker with a valentine shaped bodice and a wire hoop arranged around the hem that caused it to stand out. When, crying, she stepped out of her wet panties, he laughed and called her a baby.

The next time she saw him, he was a slender young man with a sparse new beard, shadowy, standing between his somber parents at her mother's funeral. That was important—he had known her mother! When she saw him again, she was in her freshman year at Wheaton and he was in law school. With the prodding of his mother, probably, he began to invite her out for coffee or a beer and a sandwich at the Wursthaus, a Sunday concert at the Gardner Museum. He stayed on to get an LL.D., waiting for Suzanne to grow up, as confident of his claim as the Prince watching Sleeping Beauty in her glass coffin through the brambles.

A week after her graduation, they married, the decision popular with everyone, a marriage as correct as that of the vicar's daughter in Jane Austen. She found a job in a small gallery on Newbury Street; she handled the museum prints: Chagall's flying lovers, Matisse's languid women, the horny minotaurs of Picasso's late middle age.

When Barry finished, they moved to Chicago where he took a job teaching Constitutional Law. The children were born there: Josh first; twenty months later, Amy. At twenty-four, everything that was expected of her was completed. From the beginning, she knew she had not married for love, although she did not think that would matter. She had married for security, for escape, for lack of plans, to get on with her life in the only way she knew. If she'd had a mother or an income or a room of her own. . . .

The summer between her junior and senior years she escaped long enough to take a job as a summer helper in Paris. She took courses at the Alliance Francaise four mornings a week and in the afternoon accompanied three small girls to the park.

In Paris, she learned the usual things: to eat dessert with both a fork and spoon, to eat snails, to tie a scarf a dozen ways, and make up her eyes with kohl. By the time they were supposed to leave for the country, she had fallen in love with the children's father, a smart charming man twenty years older than she who edited a prestigious medical journal. Alain Bertrand.

He had taken a room in the attic of a building on the Ile de la Cité. They met there several times a week in the early evenings. After giving her dinner—hence, the implement and eating instruction—and making love, he would return to the apartment in the Sixth, where he lived with his wife and those three little girls, and where Suzanne lived, too, except on those nights she slept alone on the Ile. The bed was under the windows and while they made love, if he placed her on top of him, something he liked very much—he told her this was the way the ancient Romans had made love— she could see the worn gargoyles and delicate buttresses of Notre Dame, lighted for the tourists. She watched the barges skim along the Seine. She was Jean Seberg and Audrey Hepburn; she had never felt so beautiful. She knew it was love that made her beautiful.

Madame always asked her how her date was the next morning, but by the time they were supposed to leave for Normandy, Madame knew—it had happened before. Suzanne was sent home early in shame. The first person she called was Barry. By the end of the summer, they were engaged.

Now, sitting in the pretty terraced garden in Berkeley, everything came flooding back. The names of the children appeared magically: Katel, Sophie, Claudine. Before, the only thing she remembered were their faces as they watched her silently packing her suitcases in the tiny bedroom off the kitchen. They had been ordered not to speak to her.

Now she knew what had she done, but then she was twenty years old and had been seduced and abandoned, like a heroine in a beloved novel by Hardy. Once home, she felt tremendous relief and gratitude to Barry. She would be faithful forever—a bad Hardy heroine trait. So she married eagerly: no fear of unleashed passion here.

The book she was writing piqued these issues of love versus marriage and her work was going badly. Since she had read it hungrily, at sixteen, almost dizzy with excitement and recognition, she had been fascinated by the opposing images of women in *Anna Karenina*. For years she theorized that all women were either Annas or Kittys. Being a Kitty herself, it was the Annas who fascinated her.

Over the years, she had known five women who left their husbands: two were writers, one was a lawyer, one was a weaver and one took photographs of brides and children. All five women had dark hair and lovers. One of them drove a vintage Porsche she maintained herself. Another cooked

game and organ meats frequently and wrote a
regular column on the heavy dark wines of Tus-
cany for an obscure food magazine. Suzanne, on
the other hand, was fair and drove a Volvo wagon
and usually got sick when she ate *ris de veau*. She
doubted she could base academic research, even
the kind she did, on a sample of five neighbors
and a handful of fictional characters.

This book was a test, a hurdle, she needed it for
tenure in this precarious market if she was going
to compete after her classically female late-start.
Her young colleagues' biological clocks may have
been ticking, but her brain was rapidly atrophy-
ing, she liked to joke, and her eyesight was going.
All day she sat in the too pink bedroom of the
rented house with her old dog and squinted
through the California sunshine into her computer screen. Everyone pointed to the spectacular
views the house offered—bays, bridges, low mountain ranges—but she could not even see her own
words.

She was trying to cover the wide windows with
poster board one morning when the phone rang.
When she finally got it, she couldn't hear anything.
She hung up and started to hammer and it rang
again. It was her husband. She had complained
that she felt alone, isolated, out of touch; Barry had
had a car phone installed to solve these problems.

Lucia didn't seem to care much for Berkeley, either: its steep walks and unleashed dogs and year round fleas, the odd sweet odors of jasmine and jacaranda. She walked a block or two and turned back, lay down, declined to proceed, even with the promise of biscotti at the cafe at the foot of the hill.

When Suzanne could not work, which was frequent, she lay on one of the slippery leather sofas in the Deco living room and closed her eyes and listened to Glenn Gould play Bach through a set of high powered quadraphonic Bose speakers. She listened and listened as if her salvation depended on it. These were recordings Gould made late in his life, when he was truly desperate, living alone, not sleeping. He couldn't perform in public anymore. He was dying spiritually and physically and he sang and hummed as he played. It was painful to witness this confession, almost too intimate, and profoundly sad and moving. In other words, it spoke directly to her condition and her belief—although she did not quite know why she felt that way—that she was dying, too.

Suzanne missed her children and knew she would be missing them for the rest of her life now. She began to think of their childhood with such fondness, it was as if it had been her own. An only urban child of busy, intellectual people—her father was a doctor with a large practice, her mother had been a social worker with a strict sense of life's purpose—Suzanne had invented the playful childhood she had wanted for herself for Josh and Amy.

At night she lay in this strange king-size plat-form bed and imagined car accidents, muggers, rapists, airplane crashes. She bought a pair of Rasta bracelets from a stand on Telegraph Avenue and tied one on each of her wrists to keep them safe, she wore t-shirts from their schools, she ritually checked their weather every morning. She developed a complicated system of changing or not changing her earrings if they were en route some-where.

She knew this was neurotic, depressive, ob-sessional. She even knew it had something to do with her mother's death, but she could not stop it. This period in her life seemed to be some kind of rehearsal, a transition, although she was hard pressed to say what this period was: empty nest, menopausal, middle-aged?

"Oh, god," laughed her friend Monique, over the phone. She was a feminist literary historian of good humor and high repute. "You sound like the heroine of this novel . . . there was this scandalous book written by a Dane at the beginning of the century about a woman like you."

"What's it called?" Suzanne asked, pen poised.

"*The Dangerous Age*," her friend intoned ominously. "She leaves a perfectly good marriage to find herself. Several of her friends follow suit and end in the worst of circumstances: alone, disgraced. At least one woman kills herself. It was quite a *succes à fou*, blamed on the burgeoning women's suffrage movement, of course. I think I can locate a copy for you. You do read German?" she said.

"Oh, that's okay, " said Suzanne. "I think I'll take an aerobics class."

Even with her children there, it was a strange Christmas in a stranger's house. She strung the ficus tree in the corner of the dining room with red and green plastic pepper lights; they ate Thai. They all watched *A Wonderful Life* on the large screen TV. Amy groaned and rolled her eyes and made gagging gestures but Suzanne wept, and could not stop. Josh watched his mother with dismay and tried to distract her with funny stories from school, while Barry opened bottles of spicy whites from the boutique vineyards down the coast.

On Christmas Day they drove to Napa where they were spending the night at the hotel where Suzanne and Barry had celebrated their anniversary the previous year. They ate a picnic lunch at the spring at Calistoga. No one else was there. The geyser, minor by any standards, took on a symbolic lack of importance. By now, Amy was deep into the latest tome by Umberto Ecco (a Christmas present from her mother) and Josh was calling his girl friend in New York, hourly. They had had to put Lucia into a kennel and Suzanne felt miserable about it.

Josh stayed on a few days after Amy left early to ski with friends in Vail. Suzanne and he perused the bookstores where she bought him a well used and sauced copy of Julia Child's *Volume I* and taught him to make a *coq au vin*. When he left she did not go to the airport. She was afraid to let him see her cry again.

Friends from Chicago visited, and colleagues of Barry's. They took them to Chez Panisse and Zuni and the small Vietnamese restaurants in Albany that bore the names of places she remembered from the war. They took a subscription to the San Francisco Opera; they toured Sonoma, they spent a weekend in Carmel, they made trips to Point Reyes and Yosemite. Barry kept toasting them on taking full advantage of things after those busy years of child rearing and career building. Now their lives could begin, he said. She felt her life was over.

Suzanne stared at the man across from her at a

table upstairs at Chez Panisse. Barry's mouth was moving up and down; bits of mesclune and raddichio were sticking to his teeth. She heard, "Me, me, me. . . . I, I, I. . . ." She noticed that his hair was seriously thinning. He had started wearing a gold chain and colored jockey shorts. She had known him since she was a child and she didn't love him.

The master bath in the rented house had a Japanese tub—you had to step down into it and then you sat up on a little marble ledge. Barry loved this tub; he loved Berkeley. He confessed weekly he had never been so happy in life. She knew he could have an offer anytime: he was a hotshot, in his prime, an expert on intellectual property with an exotic, vaguely left-wing twist that endeared him to Boalt Hall. He was certain they could come up with something for her. She might not get tenure at National College, he reminded her. He could play tennis outdoors all year, he reminded her.

"What is wrong with you, Suzanne?" he asked. "What is it, hormones, thyroid, calcium? I mean, is it this change of life stuff?"

"The dangerous age? " she asked and began to laugh a little hysterically. "It's a book," she said.

"It's wonderful here. You won't give it a chance."

"Maybe if we had come here directly from

Cambridge . . . I think I'm too old to start again."

"Well, I'm not," he said, seriously. "I'm getting younger everyday."

Was he more selfish than most of the successful men she knew? He had simply been preoccupied in those early tender years of their marriage, but he was a conscientious father—he had done a better job with Josh than with Amy. He had taken care of all of them, encouraged her to return to school and write her dissertation. He had stayed with the children once when she had given a paper at a conference in Ostend. Was their marriage worse or more boring or different than those of their friends?

People started to invite them to dinner. In this food mecca, however, where the menu outlined the early childhood of your veal chop and the lifestyle of the roast chicken, no one cooked: you ate out. Everyone's wife was a lawyer; the children were singular and small and precocious, parents were old and ambitious. One night someone took them to a party in a big house in the Flats. The smell of marijuana wafted from open windows; in the hall, people had left their Birkenstocks and Patagonia jackets in a great heap. She stared at her empty Maud Frizon pumps and worried that they might be stolen.

The furniture had been cleared from the living room, Jefferson Airplane blared on the stereo and in the room were dozens of shaking, grinding bodies, sweaty with sexual heat and energy. But these bodies were aging, grey-haired and wrinkled, heavy bellied and loose bosomed. She felt like Rip van Winkle at a graduate school party; twenty-five years had passed quietly since she fell asleep.

"Welcome to the warmth," a counterculture historian whispered in her ear as they were dancing to something slow.

"Well, the weather is much better here. . . ." she agreed.

"No, no, not the weather," he said soothingly, "the aura. It's so cold out there," he said vaguely. "I was there once."

"Maybe we met, when was that?"

"Oh, not in this life," he said, holding her close.

The exercise studio she had found had a bad floor and she hurt her feet again and again: the plantar fascia. She cracked the stress fractures she had in both feet. The orthopedist she consulted admired the flexibility of her feet. "Pretty," he said, holding her bare foot in his hand, and talked about the inevitable breakdown of the body.

She thought maybe she could have an affair with the doctor, or the historian from the time-warped party, or the landscape designer who appeared in his pick-up truck one afternoon and stayed for wine, or the aerobics instructor who was young and smooth and very gay. She wished with all her heart for her children to be small and hers again, to finish her book, to run into a familiar face at Andromico's Park and Shop, at a reading at Black Oak, at Peet's for coffee, but she never did.

5

Robert was a child of pioneers, settlers in the piney woods of East Texas, two brothers who harvested the crops before joining the Rebel troops in Henderson, returning home with pale and gentle Alabama wives. A great uncle had driven the herds north on the Chisholm trail at the age of fifteen; his sister had taken a team of horses west to California during a gold rush, under cover of night with a husband half-dead of consumption, their money tucked up in her top-knot of hair. Another uncle, a tent preacher, wrestled steers from the Red River and remembered seeing Geronimo and Quanah Parker. There were dozens of stories like this in his family, of men and women of courage and reckless action, restless, possessed by a kind of American wanderlust—from sea to shining sea.

His own father had left the farm at fourteen to find fame and fortune in the oil fields of southern California. Robert was born there in the last year of a decade that began in wild abandon and ended in despair, at the crack of noon. His mother claimed she heard the noon whistle as he came screaming into the world. He was named for his mother's father, a rancher whose tall craggy form he followed with love and admiration each summer from the time he was three until he was almost fifteen and had begun his own life in earnest.

He remembered everything: leaving in the middle of the night from the rambling stucco station in Los Angeles, the final dinners at an Italian restaurant, the stiff box of baked goods for later hanging from his wrist on a loop of red and white string, his father's winey smell and leather feel, traveling 2000 miles by train from California to East Texas.

As he grew, his mother was busy with one baby or another, the little sisters who entered his life, but never really touched it. He was a boy of five, six, seven; for three summers each time they passed through the mountains, the border that separates New Mexico from Texas, he looked out and there, at dusk, with Mexico hanging on one side, he saw perched on the top of a rocky peak a huge golden mountain lion: majestic, still. The first summer, he called out breathless to his mother, but she was busy with Ruby Sue or DeLynne and by the time she finished pinning a diaper or checking the blanket, the lion was gone, the train had moved on.

His mother smiled at him—he was truly her dear sweet boy—but he knew she did not believe him and so the next summer he learned not to call to her, tell her, and the lion was his, his alone. It was his first act of separation from his beloved mother, his first secret from her, and he savored it. Then one summer, as they passed over that mountain range, the lion was not there. It was never there again, but by then it did not matter because he did not need to see it for it to be there.

When he was 20 months old he contracted polio: the fever first, then chills, the weakness and finally paralysis. He had just learned to run, to feel confident on his own two feet in this world. He lay near death for a month in the hospital in Los Angeles. They let his mother bring him home on the condition she get a nurse for round-the-clock, and they did, a tall dusky woman, part Cherokee, Helen Vee Holmes, a Seventh Day Adventist. Helen Vee sent his father out for a long piece of flannel at the Penney's—it was black and pink check. She tore this cloth into long strips and they wet them in hot water and wrung them out tight on the handle of a broom until they were almost dry and wrapped his frail trembling lost limbs in them. Helen Vee taught his mother to make a thin gruel of potatoes in water and strain it and feed it to him round the clock, to give him some nourishment and keep him from dehydration, keep his exhausted lungs from closing up altogether. Later, he remembered, his mother would scrape a piece of steak with a big spoon and feed him the mash. When he grew a little stronger, his father made a ramp with railroad ties from the yards and there, a strong proud woman holding each hand, he learned to walk again. To strengthen him, they sent him for dancing lessons, ballet and tap, where they snapped his picture in a sailor suit and hat beneath a paper moon. They fretted and prayed and wept and saved his life: women.

When they went for a drive, his mother would tell him what she saw in the clouds. His mother saw more things in the sky, his father liked to say, than others saw on the earth. Recently, she had sent him a crumbling Bible with all the names and dates of his ancestors in a large slanted hand and purple tinted prints of the Holy Land: the Via Dolorosa filled with donkeys and faded Arabs, the Garden of Gethsemane, the Tomb of Sarah.

He remembered the tank full of water moccasins his grandfather loaned to the Baptists and he thought of those endless Sundays of bad smells: heat and wilting blowsy flowers, the ripe suit coats of the farmers, the sour breath of the old ladies who would clasp him to their damp bosoms as if to take his life away. Even now Sundays made him a little tired.

The Christmas he was eight they spent in Texas with his grandparents. When the first frost came, and a full moon, it was the time to butcher the hogs. He remembered following his grandfather into his office, a small room off the main room of the house, the big room where his grandparents slept in a massive oak bed. There were sofas and chairs in that room and the brown mahogany cabinet with the radio, it's bright face showing like the eternal flame. In the center now was a tall pine tree, weighted with tinsel and crisscrossed with strings of popcorn that he and Granny had made early in the week. There were some paper ornaments his mother had made as a girl, and bright colored glass balls from Wacker's Five and Dime Store, balls so fragile he was sure his breath could shatter them.

His grandfather took his .38 pistol out of a locked drawer, loaded it and took his hand. Outside was everyone he knew: all the farm hands and neighbors, his father and two of his brothers, the little black children he played with and their mothers. Darkies, his mother and his grandmother called them. He remembered his mother was there talking to them. She hugged him to her. Her curly dark hair was loose and he remembered how it glowed in the sharp light that was just beginning to show. She had one of the Indian pattern blankets wrapped around her; her long legs were white and bare in the cold. His sisters must have been asleep in the house.

He could see the first great hog in the pen: his hoofs had been tied to each post of the fence and his nasal cries filled the air. His grandfather raised his gun. He stood on the lower rungs of the fence, his legs spread apart like the trestle of a table. The arm with the gun was outstretched long before him, the other rested on a post of the fence. He aimed and shot the hog between his eyes.

Robert remembered he hadn't been looking and the sound of gunshot stunned him out of his reverie, long enough to catch the huge familiar form of the hog jolt, and, as suddenly, sag. Then it was dragged by the ropes and hoisted from a beam that had been erected the day before over a huge cast iron pot of boiling water, but not before it was cut open. The blood dazzled him. Parts of the hog that were prized by them were given to the cheering black helpers who speared them on waiting sticks and stuck them into the fire beneath the pot. His mother ate this, too, and he tried, but when he took a bite it was, what: too strong, too salty, or was he too sad? Something kept him from being able to swallow.

Now, sitting alone in a leather wing chair in

the library of his grand house with its leaded glass views of trees and lawn and the great grey lake, Robert couldn't remember how he got from there to here. Memories he thought lost were suddenly conjured up daily with the clarity of the omniscient and, as he thought more and more about it, it was his present life that seemed less real to him.

He had plenty of time to think. Reaching in the attic rafters for the box with the Christmas lights for Louise— their house was on the Junior League Tour again—he pulled his back, herniating two discs he had injured several years before. This time he needed surgery. He thought of Suzanne sometimes as he lay on his back during the long recovery. He liked to imagine her dancing around the dark studio; he wanted to talk to her about pain. He wanted to tell her about the nights it was so bad he could not sleep and he lay awake thinking about death for the first time since Korea. He wanted to tell her that the pain was so bad he would have crawled on his knees on cut glass to get to the hospital, that he would have had the surgery without anesthesia, just a bullet to bite. Then he could tell her his mother's story of the shooting of her grandfather when she was four, and how she hid behind a chair as they carried in the bloody body and laid him out on the dining room table.

Once, lonely, on a whim, he called Information for Suzanne's number, but there were Millers listed in Highland Park and Glencoe as well as Evanston and Wilmette and he didn't know her husband's name.

At a banking conference in Bermuda, his wife issued him an ultimatum. After 35 years of marriage, she wanted a divorce. She had waited patiently, dutifully, for the last of their three daughters to grow up. Margaret was at boarding school this fall, and she could finally think about what she wanted from life, and she wasn't sure it included him.

They were dressing for dinner and he sat on the end of his twin bed tying his shoes. Louise sat cool, confident, detached, dressed in a new linen sheath with pearl buttons and slender bone and black spectator pumps. He handed her his handkerchief, but she handed it back. Her eyes were dry.

He had met her on a blind date on a weekend leave from the Marine Corps. She was visiting a former roommate from school who was working in Washington. An engagement to the man she had been planning on marrying for most of her life had been recently broken—she never told Robert the reason. No stranger to women, he had never met anyone like Louise. He mistook her aloofness for sophistication, her unusual ideas for intelligence, and her coldness—well, he thought she was shy and would come around. Her father was the black sheep of a Chicago meat-packing family; they danced on the edge of a world of Armours and Palmers, never quite admitted but the possibility was there. Robert felt all that was lacking in his own humble origins was this cool elegant creature. She called him her diamond in the rough and said she would smooth out the edges.

She had recently entered therapy again, she told him, with a woman who had psychic powers as well as formal analytical training, who made her understand things in a way she never had before. She watched Robert closely, he was having trouble with his shoe laces. Her voice lifted with enthusiasm as she recited the woman's ability to tell personal things about the children, identify correctly the signs of both grandsons.

Louise was always looking for the true path: I am a seeker, she liked to tell people. She was always trying some new vitamin regime or soul-enriching diet, always following some new Master or guru. She visited them in trailers and store fronts and Lake Shore Drive apartments, she ran up gigantic phone bills talking to the 900 number psychics. She went to people who fell into trances, talked in tongues, made contact with her dead mother and a child they had lost at six months. She had had many lives, most of them as a member of the aristocracy; in one, Robert had been her slave. She meditated, had her Tarot read, her grandchildren's stars charted, the I Ching thrown several times a year by a local Chinese scholar, as well as serving on the flower committee at the Methodist Church.

Her quiet fury stunned him, and the fact she would keep this secret from him until now. How was she paying the therapist? he wondered. But it was her certainty that he was the problem that really impressed him. "Louise. . . ." he said, humbly.

She crossed the room and sat on the bed next to his. "I'm willing to give it one more chance. I've spoken with Melissa," she said gently now. "We're certain she can help you."

Again, he was touched by her innocence, by her pale pretty face, and he promised he would go, that he would try again, although he was not sure what he had done. He said he would see this wonderful woman as soon as they returned from the trip. Then they went to dinner.

6

Suzanne had a tumor the size of a grapefruit on her womb. It had been growing for a year.

"Didn't you notice anything?" her doctor shouted at her in disbelief. He had delivered both her children so he thought he had a right to yell at her, she supposed.

She shrugged. "I thought I was gaining weight. Or I was doing the abs work wrong, you know, I was breathing out instead of in."

Once she knew about it, she felt scared, but decided to take some pleasure in the size and shape of it. She pushed out her stomach the way she had as a little girl playing pregnant. She watched her belly grow round and hard in her leotards, her bathing suit; watched that wonderful shape of globe and pumpkin and planet beneath the disparity of her pale wrinkling face.

Her first memory was one of being sick. She was four and had been put to bed in her mother's grandmother's house, in the old grandmother's room, and she could see her ancient crinkled face, soft, expansive, hanging over the crib like the moon, her tiny mouth etched with age, speaking in a strange tongue, musical sounds, and her knobby hands passing over the crib in circles. A red ribbon was tied to the bars to ward off the evil eye, and her father, the young doctor, came into the room, laughing, saying penicillin—another magic word—and ripped off the ribbon, leaving Suzanne vulnerable and unprotected and a participant in the modern world. Her parents had assimilated with the kind of thoroughness that leaves nothing.

Now Suzanne sat still and small in a side chair as the surgeon and her husband haggled over the details across the surgeon's big mahogany desk (his office was downtown at the Medical School, not far from Barry's at the Law School). Because of the surgeon's long holiday, her operation had been postponed until September, the beginning of the academic year.

"Well, don't count on me!" Barry warned as he left her in the hall outside the busy waiting room. "The first week of classes is the worst time for me. You know that, Suzanne."

She did know that, of course, having to shuffle her own heavy teaching load.

Because of Barry's schedule, Monique drove her to the hospital in the early morning hours. Monique

stayed with her until they took her down to surgery and she was there when they brought Suzanne
back to her room. A week later, Suzanne took a
taxi home. Lucia was so thrilled to see her she
could not stop licking her face and lifting her paw
for Suzanne to shake. She refused to go out into
the small side yard until Suzanne came with her,
slumping onto an uncushioned chaise until Lucia
returned from her tour of the bushes. Then they
dragged up the stairs. Barry had not made the bed.
The sheets needed to be changed and she could
smell him on all the pillow cases, but she pushed
aside the crumpled sheets and pillows and, dressed,
just lay there gratefully for a long time.

The tumor had been so large and distended,
and her uterus so soft and strange, they feared that
she was pregnant, that there was a fetus in there,
and so they cut it open to see before they cut it
out. This fact, when they told her, made her sad,
sadder than anything, a mistaken pregnancy at this
point in her life; the end of her life, she was certain now. For weeks and weeks after she came
home, she lay in the bathtub and cried for this
loss: the loss of her missing children, the loss of
their former home, the source of her former
power, her fertility, youth, the loss of this part of
her life.

At the hospital, she had agreed to be part of a

study of hysterectomy patients, comparing their abrupt adjustment to menopause with women going through it in a more leisurely way. Each month a nursing student who had been assigned to her would call and recite an alphabetical list of adverbs to describe possible feelings. Suzanne was supposed to stop her when the word applied. Invariably, the student called at dinner time, when Suzanne was rushed and distracted, and this disembodied voice over the phone, low and breathy, childlike and mildly seductive, took on the sensation of a strange interlude, the interruption of an obscene caller.

"Addled . . . adjusted, adventurous . . . now just stop me, Mrs. Miller, when you want . . . alienated, anticipatory, anxious, appreciative. . . ."

"Wait, anxious," Suzanne said. "And . . . anticipatory. . . ."

She was asked, in this same hushed voice, about her sex drive—this was to be rated on a scale of one to five—and her need to masturbate, her feelings about her thighs and the appearance of her vagina. The student sounded so young and unsure of herself, the whole process seemed vaguely off-color, hilarious and touching.

It reminded Suzanne of those early feminist meetings where they'd lie on their backs on a table in someone's family room and, following the lead of a visitor from headquarters, peek inside themselves with a speculum. Suzanne always declined her turn. Inside herself meant her soul, as far as she was concerned, and she didn't think it was pink or magenta, smooth or striated.

It was November before she made it to the exercise class again. In the hall, before the studio opened, she saw Robert waiting. She remembered looking for his picture in the field house in Berkeley among the display of trophies and team photographs. She found him, too: he had shiny black hair with one curl lost and spiraling down his forehead. She had meant to send him a post-card of Sproul Plaza.

She didn't think he recognized her. In a gesture of self-inflicted punishment—classic female castration—Suzanne had chopped off her hair. She thought it would be easier to care for, although she should have known the real reasons, having studied enough about women's haircuts in fairy tales, religious orders and rituals; childhood heroines, rebellious flappers and gift-giving wives. (She could have annotated this: Jo March in *Little Women*, Beatrice in the Scott Fitzgerald story and the wife in *The Gift of the Magi*, by O. Henry.)

The short hair frustrated her: it would not cooperate, it would not stay in the black or pink elastics. The ends popped out of a miniature pony tail and, at some point, before the end of the class, she just let it out, causing her fractured hair to fly around her puffy pale face.

Robert watched this and he watched her talk to people. She seemed different, humbler, more friendly, like someone who has survived a terrible lonely experience, a child's death, or being held hostage.

"I had surgery in September," she said, leaning heavily against the wall. "A big operation. I feel dead."

He was bigger than she remembered—he seemed huge, in fact, and very handsome. Standing beside him, she felt very young, small, fragile, feminine. These were things she had not felt for a long time, although she knew some of them were still true. She had a sudden desire to collapse against him. She remembered. "How's your back?"

"Well, I hurt it again." He put his head back and laughed. "I had to have an operation this time."

"Oh no. I broke my feet, too. You should have seen the x-rays, these thin white lines. They're a mass of fractures. I'm falling apart."

"No, you're not." He smiled. She seemed so soft to him, so sad, with that edge gone, the sureness. "How often do you do this?"

"Six times a week, sometimes seven."

"Do you think you should do it that much?"

"I'm heavy and I'm out of shape. I hate being out of shape."

"You should allow your body to heal," he said. "Don't rush it."

"I'm very impatient with my so-called body," she said. "And I'm always in a terrible hurry."

He was touched by her confession. He wondered what the surgery was, a big operation at mid-life. A hysterectomy, he supposed, his wife had had one about then.

She started to come earlier, to hang out in the back, to talk to him. She noticed how he would just stand there, relaxed against the back wall and people would come to him. He seemed a beacon, a father, he had the calm of a priest bestowing a blessing on his congregation. He told her they were announcing the engagement of his oldest daughter, Eleanor, his Nell, at Thanksgiving.

"How many are there?" Suzanne asked.

He answered easily and with great pleasure. His middle daughter, Anne, was married to a lawyer in Boston; they had two little boys. She had been an accomplished pianist and sang in the church choir and was renovating an old house they had recently moved into in Wellesley. The bride-to-be, Nell, lived in an apartment in Old Town and was a broker on the Commodities Exchange. The youngest, Margaret—she was called Mags—was in boarding school in the East.

"There are always three sisters," said Suzanne.

For a reason he didn't know, he suddenly imagined Suzanne with his daughters. He wondered how she would handle them. He wanted to warn her that three sisters made for a lot of tears and jealousies and gossip.

But all she said was, "Chekov. Great art doesn't lie."

He shouldn't have worried about this frightening off Suzanne, it appealed deeply to her literary imagination. She saw the groaning polished sideboard, Robert in a needlepoint vest and fine cravat, brandishing his steel and blade over the broad and crusty bird, the pretty blond wife in spectator pumps, a pink apron tied over her shirt waist dress, smiling at his side—a cross between a Dickens feast and a Norman Rockwell tableau. He had to have a blond wife, she thought, in fact they were all blondes, she was sure, the daughters, too, sorority girls out of a Fifties' Breck shampoo ad.

"You have two children?" Robert asked politely.

She answered sparely, unusually, she didn't want to talk about them for a change. "Yes, I have a son and a daughter. Amy's still in college, Josh is in law school."

"You know, there was something I wanted to ask you. I was looking through your book again," he said. Actually, he had rescued it from a box intended for the church book sale, Louise's charity event of the coming season.

"Oh, that." Suzanne shrugged, almost embarrassed. "I should have another one by now. I've been working on a new book, but there's something wrong with it."

"Do you really believe that?" he asked.

"Believe what?"

"What you say in your book, that men treat women like that. That they take advantage of them, abuse them sexually."

"Yes. And that women trade that—sex—for respectability, position."

"Is your marriage like that?"

She looked at him carefully. "In a way," she said. "I married too young. I had to get away from home, my mother was dead, I wasn't really welcome in my father's new life. My husband was ready to marry—he's older by five years—and I didn't know what to do, so we married. We made a deal. He wouldn't see it that way, but it's true. What is your marriage like?"

"My marriage is like a gigantic institution," he said. "It's like a corporation, a business."

"But no love?"

"No, there hasn't been any love for a long time," he said. "I lead a monastic life."

Christmas shopping at Field's, Suzanne found herself in the lingerie department. Looking through racks of lacy things, she grabbed a black lace bustier, a bra and panties in the deepest sea green, the nipples covered in taut lace flowers and a slip of a night gown, silk with the tiniest straps. She had never owned things like this in her life. She hid them in tissue in a desk drawer tucked in with a heart-shaped rose-soaked sachet she also purchased. She began to use thick imported creams for her thighs and her breasts, her neck. Sometimes, bored, sad, she would try on her underwear and pose in the mirror in her study, but she didn't wear it anywhere else.

After Christmas, she attended a cocktail party at the Modern Language Association meetings being held at the Palmer House. As she expected, she ran into a former professor whom she had known well enough to flirt with on and off over the years. She was slightly drunk and rather unhappy and she knew she looked pretty in a new dress.

"There's a man in my exercise class who likes me," she confided. "He's a banker."

"A banker?"

"I'm trying to decide whether to have an affair with him. What do you think I should do? He drives a big black Mercedes. I'm not sure I could have an affair with a man who drives a car like that."

"It might be fun for you, dear, to slip off to the Holiday Inn, east of Edens, or wherever people go out here."

"East of Edens is the Lake, Peter," she said glumly.

"Ah, yes." He looked distracted, as if he were looking for escape.

Suzanne grabbed his arm. "It isn't just about sex," she said fiercely.

"Of course not," he said soothingly.

"I want a real man. I want a man I can talk to, a man whose lap I can climb into and whisper stories in his ear, a man I can take care of and who will take of me. I want a man I can talk dirty to and a man I can travel with and squeeze oranges for. . . ."

"Frankly, my dear," he said, "most of the men I know make their own juice."

On New Year's Eve at their class, lined up at the water fountain, Suzanne gave Robert a kiss.

"Happy New Year," she said, and extended her hand and kissed him on the cheek.

"Thank you," he said, surprised. He took her

hand and held it for a minute.

His hand felt large and cool to her and his cheek where she kissed it was slightly rough. It felt strange, his cheek and his thick brush-cut hair and the faint smell of his after-shave, citrusy, unfamiliar, and there was a sensation of passion, something stirring she hadn't felt in so long she could barely recognize it.

He had cooked his traditional New Year's Day dinner, he told her: black eyed peas and corn bread, a ham, ambrosia salad. "The peas are supposed to bring you good luck."

"Happiness?" Suzanne asked.

"Not as far as I know, just one day of luck for each one you eat."

"Look," she said. "Do you think maybe we could go somewhere and have coffee sometime and talk. Do you think that would be possible?"

"Yes, it's possible. What about this Saturday, after class?"

"Whoa," she said, then laughed. "Watch, I'll be sick or something Saturday."

"You'll be there," he said.

They sat in his big car. He had parked a mile from the Fitness Center behind a gigantic corporate campus in a lot that during the week held the hundred cars of the employees of a health insurance company. Today it was empty.

Robert looked directly ahead, out the windshield, and outlined a life for her as straight as a Midwestern highway. He talked about growing up in Bakersfield and his father who had worked in the oil fields, and then for the railroad. His family had been in this country so long, he said, no one knew exactly when they came here, but they were there, almost from the beginning. He took her hands, both of them, in one of his. "They're cold, sweetheart," he said. "Let me warm them."

He talked about being an athlete and about football and the Marines and Korea and the chronology of the births of his children and the cities where they had been born. He told her they had lost a baby, too, the only boy, when he was six months old, and how he suffered a loss of faith that had never returned. He believed in something bigger than himself, he said, but he didn't go to church anymore.

She asked him about his wife. He told her how much in love with her he had been, how he had put her on a pedestal. "That was probably the problem," he said, and described how it began to change 15 years ago with the birth of their youngest child and had never been good at all since then. He leaned forward to kiss her, gently at first, as if he was not sure she was even there, and she felt not there, very small and very young, shy. Then he pressed her to him and kissed her with his mouth and she wrapped her arms around his neck and touched his face with her warmed hands.

He called her love. He told her he had been faithful to his wife all these years. He said he didn't know what she had in mind, he wanted some friendship and a little comfort, the kind you can only get from a woman.

She didn't talk much, but watched him. She put her hand on the sleeve of his jacket and left it there while he talked. When he talked about his journey from boyhood it was as if it were an epic tale, as if he had traveled from China on a tall ship with wide high sails. It made her think of the houses she had seen on a trip to Egypt, the way the walls were decorated with the scenes of the owner's pilgrimage to Mecca. There, bold and primitive as the drawings of a school child, was the man and his house, his family waving good-bye, the plane and boats that took him there, the dome of the great Mosque; camels, cars. She knew everyone's life was really a record of this journey and that it was the only story we have to tell. She was glad to hear his, but she couldn't think of a thing to say herself.

She was wearing an old cape of heavy loden

cloth with suede buttons and a short collar. She let it fall open and he undid the buttons of her sweater and pulled it open and looked at her breasts in the new lace brassiere she had fastened with shaking hands in the locker room after the exercise class. It was very fine, French, and a color neither green or blue. The name of the model of the brassiere was Josephine, for Napoleon's love. She told him that.

Robert touched her breasts through the lace and he kissed her and he looked at her and smiled. She leaned her head back on the seat of the car, her mouth opened slightly, and then he buttoned her sweater back up and covered her up with her cloak the way he would have his daughters when they were small.

Later he told her, "I brought you along in that car, sweetheart. You come on cocky, but I could tell you were shy, inexperienced, and so I brought you along slowly."

7

Unusual for February, mild, sunshine, a real thaw; the air was soft, the light tawny. Guests in from New York for the week-end—a friend from graduate school, Abigail Mandel and her husband and her little girl. Twenty were coming for dinner to meet them. She and Abby drank tea in her big white kitchen.

"I love this house," Abby said. "What a great life you have, Suzanne."

"I don't know."

"Are you all right?" This was said thoughtfully, uncritically.

"I'm just tired. I haven't been sleeping well at all."

"You look fine—thin, but rather radiant."

"It's a beautiful day. . . ."

"Yes, shall we go for a walk?"

"Someone . . . a man I know . . . I know of a wedding at the church just up the street . . . that big white church near the Lake . . . a fancy wedding, the bride in white, nine bridesmaids. I thought Katie would like that."

"I said we'd get some ice cream."

"Oh, we'll do that, too. Yes, Kate? Shall we?"

They found a place discreetly across from the church—she was afraid to be too close to him. Would she call out his name, faint? No, it was entirely innocent, her need for him, to see him, to watch him walk with his daughter on his arm, share his pride, his love—could she share these things? The cars drove up at last: he was in the wide back seat of the limo with his daughter Nell, his hand wrapped around hers. The bride was smiling, waving gaily over her shoulder to a friend. She noticed the three of them, too, and waved to Kate. Suzanne knew Nell had gone to school in this town; in the years to come her children would be christened here.

Robert was formal, tender, concerned. He extended his arm to help her out of the car. Her dress was a cloud—she would never be this beautiful again. Another daughter rushed down the steps holding the bouquet, bending to straighten the bride's short train. She kissed her father, too. (Suzanne stared at Robert's wife and quickly compared herself to her— his wife was taller, blonde, older, handsome and sure of herself—but how could she? This woman and she were like the apples and oranges her grammar school teachers

78

insisted could not be added together.)

The wedding party gathered on the steps in the bright winter sun, pausing, posing, squinting into the camera. Late comers hurried up the steps. The bride was chatty, happy. Robert's wife looked at her watch, caught his attention and he nodded in agreement, gestured to the photographer.

As he turned to enter the open door of the church, he spotted Suzanne, small, intense, holding the hand of a child and the tightened leash of her old dog. He raised a hand.

That night she wore a slim red belt with a large silver heart-shaped buckle because she could not wear her heart on her sleeve. Her arms hung white and useless by her sides.

"You have beautiful skin," he had told her a few days earlier, and she had laughed and said, "I show you only the best parts." But what she meant to say was, with him, for him, she was always the best she could be.

She flashed her bare arms and pranced on a pair of slender red shoes on high thin heels, a fan of suede and three shiny buttons on the vamp.

"Fuck me shoes," Monique said, as she came into the house. "There are two kinds of shoes in the world, darling, fuck you shoes and fuck me shoes, and those are definitely the latter."

Empowered, Suzanne strutted with a loose gait learned from women in the movies—Lauren Bacall, Marlene Dietrich— the walk of women much longer-legged than she, and hugged her male guests, her friends, let them embrace her, leave their hands on her shoulders, back, aware of her hollows, her bones, curves, aware of her need to be touched and held. She understood now why she had always allowed this embracing— encouraged it—her need to play pretty child for them for an evening, although when it was over, she was back in the house of the dull distant king and all her songs and stories and dances would not turn his head because he was on to her, knew she was not obedient, well-behaved, a proper wife. This was the fable at the heart of her marriage.

All evening she thought of Robert: now he's receiving his guests, now he's kissing the women, now he's dancing with the bride. Now she was lighting the candles, now she was greeting her guests. Could he feel her from where he was, a mile from this house? She had made *gravlax*, and sliced it very thin on a slight angle. She served it with a creamy mustard sauce and potatoes boiled with dill and a sharp cucumber salad. There was dark bread and Swedish crisp bread to eat with caraway cheese; dark beer and cold aquavit. She imagined feeding this to Robert, serving it on her heavy Danish silver, the spiked fork and flat fish knife, balancing potato and fish and sauce so their tastes and textures entered your mouth and mingled at once. Twenty years before, they had spent a sabbatical year in Stockholm where Barry taught American Constitutional Law to the skeptical Swedes—a strange vibrant time that had taken on the extremes of light and dark of a Bergman film, by now, leaving only a penchant for cold fish, the trick of massing fat candles on huge trays and the acquisition of several dozen bright wood Christmas ornaments in the shapes of hearts and pigs and apples. She thought suddenly of her husband's Swedish colleagues: Sven, Hans, Lars, brooding, intense, unfaithful men. How young and confident they had all been then. Last Fall someone called to tell them Sven was dead.

For dessert she had baked two cheesecakes, light and dark again: one chocolate with a dusting of powdered sugar and cocoa, the other plain and covered with blood oranges, arranged in concentric circles like the sun. These recipes were the legacy from her mother's grandmother. Her mother had told her the grandmother had refused to give them to her for ten years until she was certain the marriage would last. Suzanne wondered what her mother would make of her behavior; how she wished she were alive. She needed her badly now.

What a mad woman she had been this week-
end—cooking, cleaning, making up the beds for
her guests, running, rushing through these things
rote. These things she had been doing for so many
years now, doing so well, she did not even think
about them or enjoy them anymore. All week-
end she had walked in circles and thought,
Enough! Enough! She didn't think she could live
like this another minute. She must make plans
soon. She imagined a woman in a fairy tale who
could never leave her husband because there was
always one more social obligation, one more event,
one more party or plan, and on it went until one
day she died. Just an hour before, she had heard
Barry accept a dinner invitation for two weeks
from tonight and there was a trip to Paris and the
Rhone being planned in the spring, and she
needed to confirm the hotel rooms for a parent's
weekend at Amy's school.

Late, the dinner guests gone, the dishes put away,
Barry asleep, she wandered into the street to walk
Lucia and imagined Robert driving by in his big
car. He stops for one second in her driveway and
they embrace, or he rushes past, a blur with the
windows rolled up, and she is left speechless, help-
less, unable to call out to him. She looked at the
winter night sky and wished for him to come to

her, wished for his love, sent her love through the sky to him, fourteen miles up the winding lake road. She pointed out to her dog the only two constellations she could identify: The Big Dipper and Orion's Belt.

Everyone asleep, Robert was locking doors, checking lights. He listened at the bedroom doors where his children were sleeping—strange these days to have them with him. He pulled the covers over the little grandsons asleep in the bed that had been their mother's. He thought of the daughter who lay with her new husband at the hotel where the reception had been held. He thought of the hot summer nights in Texas, nights of no breeze, only the thick heat turned down a notch from day; how his grandfather, huge to him as a boy of six or seven, dressed in the pale cotton nightshirt he wore, would go from room to room in the middle of the night with an enormous tin pitcher filled to the wide-lipped spout with ice water. His grandfather would shake him awake long enough to hand him a tall beaded glass before going on to the next room and the next to perform the same errand of mercy, and then Robert would nestle down next to one boy cousin or another, finding the fresh linen sheet with his feet, and wrap it over his feet and the bottoms of his legs. He still slept this way.

He remembered the night his oldest sister was born. He had been asleep on the screened porch of his grandfather's house. And men were pacing—his father and his grandfather, an uncle— there were men's voices, the screen door slamming again and again in the night and then the news, whispered to the sleeping boy in the middle of the night that he has a sister, a girl child. Whose child was that with Suzanne today? He let himself think of his little love, her small white face at the church. He did not know how she slept: on her back or stomach, curled up, stretched out. He imagined her pale arms arranged in an arch above her bright tangled hair.

He got into his narrow bed, alone, and reached for the bed light and prayed he would fall asleep quickly, although he knew he would not. He rarely fell asleep easily anymore and would need his pipe, a hot bath, some cookies and a glass of milk, and the parts of the Trib he hadn't read that morning.

The reading light in the guest room was on. Suzanne suspected they were making love—it was a recent, rather passionate second marriage. She stepped into the front hall and locked the heavy front door. She didn't sleep, she hadn't slept since her surgery in September. Someone tonight told her it was fluctuating hormones.

Leaning over the kitchen sink, she peeled a blood orange, the juice staining her hands red, and she thought of her monthly bleeding, so untimely stopped, gone forever, the end of so much for her, gone, gone: her children, her youth, ended with the flick of a knife. So much of her gone, she felt like a hollow woman, skin and bone until Robert had entered to give her new life. She needed him to fill her; she wanted to hang on to him, to pull on his thick hair and let him ride her all the way home.

Sunday, she made a large brunch for her guests, scrambling a dozen eggs with leftover salmon, frying last night's boiled potatoes, toasting the day-old French bread. Everyone was hung over, sleepy; the weather returned to its appropriate dreariness; Kate needed to be entertained. Suzanne and Abby took her for a long walk along the Lake and Abby confided her problems with a book she was completing on Osip Mandelstam. She stopped to recite, in Russian, then in English, some lines of his about childhood and the night sky and heaven beating down.

Suzanne was stunned by the poem, the sudden recitation, the words and her thoughts outside the night before and she began to talk about Robert

Parrish for the first time to anyone, slowly, stilt-edly, almost in a whisper. "I think I'm falling in love. . . ," she said, "a man I met in my exercise class. . . ."

"Was that his daughter's wedding?" smart Abby asked.

"Yes," Suzanne confessed and then, embarrassed, laughed and blushed.

"You seemed mighty determined to get there," Abby said, then asked softly, "What will you do?"

"I don't know. I love him. I hadn't even real-ized how much until now, until I told you. I love him," she said again, "I'm in love with him."

"Will you leave Barry?" Abby asked, her voice low and flat.

"I think I have to."

"I wish you wouldn't."

"What will we do with all the stuff?" Suzanne wondered out loud. "There's so much stuff."

"I don't know," Abby said. "Oh, god, Suzanne, do you have to do this?"

They walked back in silence.

Suzanne made her weekly phone calls to her children while Abby went upstairs to pack. Nei-ther of them was in and she left brief messages after their frenetic jazzy ones, reminding Amy to get her passport pictures made and Josh to make a dentist appointment during his spring break. They ordered in Chinese food and ate with chop sticks. Kate sat on Barry's lap and he held her little hand in his to show her how and Suzanne thought what a nice man he could be. Just last week he had told her that she was the only one in his life he loved. Oh, not now, she thought, but said lightly, "Don't be silly, you love your children. And the dog."

"Oh, no," he said, "you taught me how to love the dog."

She knew that probably some people would hate her or at least not understand her; she feared Joshua would not forgive her.

They put their guests in an airport limo to catch the last flight out of O'Hare for New York. Abby ran down the steps of the house without looking back. Like a woman fleeing a disaster, Suzanne thought, don't look back or you will turn to salt. Snow clouds appeared.

Now that it was ending, she wandered through the broad high ceiling rooms of her house, admiring them, as if she were a stranger or a traveler, fondling things, moving them around dreamily, like the unrelated pieces in a surrealist canvas. She ran her hands over the chrome and leather furniture, the long library table from

London, odds and ends acquired in second hand shops, at auction, on trips abroad, from her mother-in-law's stuffed Brookline house when they moved her to a nursing home. Posters on every wall recorded art exhibitions visited over two decades: New York, Chicago, Boston, Rome, Florence, Paris, Basel. Family pictures, post-cards from friends cluttered fireplace mantels, mirror edges, the doors of the two refrigerators, window panes. Thousands of shelved and shoved and piled books traced her academic and spiritual life from college days to the present. Her children's baby shoes and her last *pointe* shoes hung from a hook in her study. On the piano in the downstairs hall, her daughter Amy's music was open to the last piece she learned, practiced seven years before, when she gave up music for field hockey: a Beethoven sonatina.

She had started wearing her children's cast-off clothes: Josh's balley sweater from Lord's cricket field, his boy-sized flannel ski pajamas with astro-nauts, a boiled wool Austrian jacket of Amy's from the fifth grade. She found a pair of earrings, metal hoops with plastic colored beads in the pocket, and wore them for a week. At night she'd awaken at three or four and wander into one of her children's empty rooms and sleep in their beds: Amy's four-poster or Josh's bunk beds, still stacked, the faded Snoopy sheets freshly washed and made up to accommodate a sleep-over friend of ten or eleven. Sometimes she threw the I Ching with a set of antique coins she bought in San Francisco's Chinatown the year before, hoping the elliptical warnings and promises of mountains and lakes would help her find her way.

She was exhausted by this deception, the restriction, these rules of conduct. She and Robert met three times a week, grabbing an extra hour before or after the class. They parked behind a rusting snow plow in the parking lot they thought of as theirs. Robert had the excuse of late phone calls, meetings, traffic; Suzanne said she was giving student conferences, doing errands, last minute grocery shopping. She began to rely on take-out meals she disguised and served in her own pots and casseroles.

Later, when Barry expressed amazement at the chain of events that changed his life, he would say to friends that he never noticed a thing different or out of the usual. She could have pointed to new perfume, a change of hairstyle, frequently shaved legs and armpits, breath mints, loss of appetite and the dozens and dozens of aluminum pans and plastic containers from the Peking Inn, the Chicken Shack, Gino's pizza and Dominick's deli counter piling up in their kitchen cabinets.

Here was a pale, aging woman, her heart aching with deceit, with what she needed to do next. She had thought she would have an affair, that it might heal her, lighten her, give her pleasure. She had not planned on falling in love, but now she knew that she had known nothing about herself when this started.

One night, wandering through the house, she glimpsed a deer in the moonlight, grazing through the snow in her neighbor's yard. It seemed impossible, an illusion, an omen of some sort. The next morning when she got to school, she overheard some of the teachers complaining that traffic had been backed up by a dead doe in the middle of Sheridan Road.

PART II

8

A time without weather; they are hidden out, comfy, in love, learning about each other's needs and desires like explorers on a Polar mission. The carriage house he rents has a wood stove in the main room and nightly they burn huge pine cones Suzanne finds around the property, and the ash and cherry logs the owner leaves on the back porch. Robert cooks for them: chicken breasts with artichoke hearts, chili, sausages with peppers; coleslaw of his own invention, the cabbage sliced very thin and tossed in heavy green oil, a little wine vinegar and crusted with heavy pepper. He squeezes half a lemon over a mound of vanilla ice cream and shows her how it makes crystalline tracks in the smooth slopes.

She cooks for him: risotto with dried porcini, linguine with clam sauce—why is everything she makes Italian? They share his big white apron, she wears jeans and tiny sweaters, and they walk obliviously barefoot on the icy tile floors. They do the dishes together: he hands them to her. She puts her hands in his back jeans pockets and presses against him at the sink. She stands on his feet and they dance to country-western music on an old portable radio liberated from one of his grown daughter's rooms. He serves her tenderly, tears off pieces of bread, feeds her bits of food as if she is his child, his patient, his prisoner.

After dinner, she sits on his lap on the modern white sofa that is the only real piece of furniture in the room, straddles him, her legs on either side, rests her hands on his shoulders. He tells her stories about the Texas town where he spent his boyhood summers. He talks about his grandfather's experiments with watermelons, how each afternoon a dozen of them would be brought up from the cellar, the heart scooped out for eating, the seeds collected from the best ones for planting the next season.

She tells him that her mother's grandfather, a Polish Jew, sprinkled salt on his watermelon, and how she tried to plant the seeds in the dry Boston soil when she was a little girl, and how on hot summer nights they would drive way out and buy a watermelon from a black man off the bed of his truck. She says they had the same childhood: grandfathers and summer nights and watermelon, only in different places. She believes this, that they are connected way back.

He says if they had only had an affair she would have never heard his stories. But she knows this is not true. He needs to tell them, he is remembering them for the first time in many years, and she needs to hear them because she needs to fill in the years without him. And she loves stories. Her own life takes place in a more recent past and has to do with travel or raising children, her mother's death. Sometimes she finds herself telling him a story by Chekhov, *The Lady and the Lapdog*, or outlining the plot of *King Lear*, as if her own life is so much less imaginative than his. Like her sister, Scheherezade, she must cast about each night for better and better stories.

She imagines the affair they might have had, once or twice a week, meeting in a bleak motel room for an hour or two. He would have told her the stories after sex because they would have made love hungrily as they arrived. She knows how he looks after making love, stretched out on his back, his big handsome head back, relaxed, remembering, leisurely, laughing out loud with memory: "Baby, have I told you about. . . ?" And how she looks, lying on her stomach, the sheet wound carelessly around her legs, her ass, hugging a pillow, raised slightly on her elbows so the tops of her breasts are exposed. She pushes a slice of damp matted hair off her cheek in a not entirely unstudied gesture. But what is this, if it isn't an affair? She is afraid to ask and never does.

He calls her as soon as he gets home from work, greets her at the door as she arrives, flushed, with a container of sauce or a bunch of the first daffodils or iris, croissants or bread, oyster mushrooms from the fish store.

"Shall we take a nap, baby?" he asks as he helps her out of her coat.

And she yawns every time. "Oh, that would be good," she says.

After dinner, he smokes a cigar. He shows her how to clip the end with his silver cutter and push a wooden match through the tip. He holds it close to his ear and rolls it lightly between his middle finger and thumb. All cigars are not alike, he instructs her, this batch is a little looser, or tighter. His cigar-makers, a venerable Dutch firm, fled from Cuba to the Dominican Republic. She sees them as in an old photograph, stained the color of tobacco, lined up at long benches in freshly ironed cotton sports shirts, their wide collars open like wings, like Breton caps, their mustachios bright with brilliantine. Robert's cigars come from a shop off LaSalle Street and after he transfers them to his humidor, each time, he solemnly hands her the empty box. "Can you use this? " he always asks.

Back in the fourth grade she could have. In the fourth grade it was the pencil case of choice, and each time she opens one of Robert's, the heavy boskey odor that escapes reminds her in a single blow exactly the way hers looked: Number 2 pencils with chewed yellow skins, a fat gummy eraser, a six inch ruler, a pencil sharpener shaped like a globe, a compass with a stub of pencil, a cheap fountain pen with *faux* marbling and cartridges of peacock blue ink. She dotted her i's with hearts an entire grade.

When he draws on his cigar, it takes her so far back in childhood, it becomes the endless Sunday of a family visit in the Fifties. Fur coats—sealskin, beaver, soft sad animals, endangered now, who gave up their lives so the women in her family could keep warm in a Boston winter— piled up on her parents' bed. The women are in the kitchen with the perking coffee pot and in the living room sit her mother's handsome uncles, public men with dulcet voices and pinkie rings, their large silver heads tilted back to suck on a White Owl or a Dutch Master—her first encounter with Rembrandt takes place inside a cigar box. It is dusk and she is curled in a big lap, comforted, cherished, held in an easy way.

Everything he does seems familiar to her; everything he does seems sexual to her: oiling and seasoning a slab of beef, sharpening his knives, shining shoes, squeezing lemons. Everything about his life is intensely masculine, ritualistic. It resembles the order of a priest preparing the host, that high seriousness, that care. He makes the coffee before they go to bed, setting the timer carefully, measuring water and beans.

They take a bath together in an old claw-footed tub in the center of the big bathroom. She scrubs his back with a loofah; she dives under water and takes him in her mouth, blowing bubbles, coming up for air. His wet cock is tasteless, all texture, smooth, like a long lovely eel. Afterward, he dries her thoroughly—crevices—with a soft pink towel; he squeezes toothpaste on her toothbrush.

They stand next to each other in front of the mirror, a towel wrapped around her waist, he is in pajamas bottoms. She holds a breast in each hand. "See," she says, "this one's bigger. It grew first. My mother said the other would catch up, but it didn't."

"Honey, they're like shoes," he says soothingly. "The right and the left can never be the same. Over the years, polishing them, rubbing them, you get to know their differences, you can tell when you touch the surface, right away, which is which."

He holds her and calls her names she could not have imagined: his bunny, his little love, his lollipop. "Oh, baby," he says, just before sleep, as he turns over, "put that beautiful ass next to me, put your big fanny there, where's my cushion, baby?"

She awakens suddenly in the middle of night, unsure of where she is. Always in the first moment she thinks she is back in the big house where she lived for years with her husband and her children and, for one second, aches with the loss, remembers the way one gracious room opened into another, the way the light filtered up the curved staircase and through the Palladium window, the way her dog slept on a pillow beside her, her bed table stacked with new books and a small gilt travel clock that had been her mother's. Most of her clothes are still in the closets.

Sometimes she feels the way she did at ten and eleven, at sleep-over parties, when about two or three in the morning, unable to go to sleep on someone's cold smelly rec room floor, she wanted desperately to sneak out and go home to her mother's clean house, to sleep in her own lovely bed. Sometimes it is too rich, too strange; she looses courage fast in the middle of the night.

But then, to awaken and see he is there—the bony tips of his shoulders, his huge hands, the bristle on his cheek, an ear, the top of his thick hair matted by the pillow— to hear his breathing, is more comforting than anything she has ever known except when she would be jolted from sleep by the hungry cries of her babies on winter nights. Suddenly awake in a cold house, she would feel that sack of bone and skin, the smooth sweet-smelling head under her chin, pulling on her breast, the little sucking sounds, the faint breathing, the sweet sour smell of her own milk, bluish, thin.

But now his eyes open slightly and she is home, and her heart leaps that he will roll over and lift her slightly to get his arms around her, and push her against his knee, and she will begin to rub against it.

"Oh, honey," he murmurs, half asleep, "your little motor's roaring."

"I can't help it," she whispers, pressing his knee between her bare thighs.

His big hands enfold a thigh each; his hands on her thighs appear as lush and formal as marble. He murmurs promises of sex—sucking, fucking—he says he will drink his morning coffee while she sucks his cock. She asks him to rest his head on her pussy and stroke the insides of her thighs.

His arms are wrapped around her waist, her arms are around his neck. She tells him now she is taller than he, when they lie like this, he is her baby. She smooths his forehead, his thick silvered hair, she touches the sharp bony places on his shoulders, she calls them his hangers. He kisses her throat, her breasts. She knows this is the greatest happiness she will ever know and that there is nothing else but this—this holding and stroking, the sweet mumbling in the middle of the night— it is worth everything to be simply here with him.

"I have to sleep, baby," he says, "I have to go to work tomorrow."

"I know," she sighs, and soon she is asleep, too.

She loves the way his voice changes as he begins: lowers, softens, his voice strokes her at the same time as his hands begin their descent, and she is lost in the wilderness of her own needs, needs created by him, choreographed by him, satisfied only by him. During the day, she thinks of his hands touching her, finding their own true place, remembers as his fingers spread apart the soft hairs on her lips, her gown lifting above her head as he caresses her breasts, nipples.

"Don't get my pajamas wet, honey," he says and she moans and moves. "Oh, baby," he says, "get them wet, spread it all over me," and she presses against him.

"Am I wet?" she always asks. "Am I wet enough?"

"Oh, honey," he laughs, "what do you think?

You're dripping."

"What can I do for you?" she asks. "Should I kiss you there?"

"That would be nice, baby," he says, and his weight shifts in anticipation.

She pulls the tie on his pajama bottoms and finds that part of him, soft at first, the skin sweet and soft before it becomes so hard and taut, purple, deepening.

He is purple, she says, the color of the black iris the Dutch prized. He says she is pink everywhere, inside her nostrils, the flush of her neck, her cheeks, ass, the triangle above her breasts when she comes and comes and comes. She finds him with her hands, her mouth, her hair brushes over his stomach and cock. He reaches down to pull her hair, touch it, caress it, and his hands move down to her. She grasps his hand, presses her legs together, moves.

She lives for night, the rest is a blur: details of divorce, settlement, sorting out papers, a lifetime of insurance papers, income taxes, securities and bonds, household goods, furniture. She spends the days talking on the phone to her lawyer, to her brave children away at school; she has sad lunches with confused friends; her husband leaves angry messages on her machine. She cannot work; she teaches her classes in the most perfunctory way.

One day she begins a lecture in tears and cannot continue. Each time she is frightened she will tell her story instead of those of Anna or Agatha and Catherine of Siena, Cinderella and Emma Bovary, Pocahantas. Nothing makes sense except night in this bed, lying next to this man. She prays he will awaken, that he will turn to her, touch her, talk to her, hold her, take her, press her, rub her, penetrate her, move her, love her.

"Sit on me, baby," he says, "sit up on me."

And it begins. She sits up and he pushes himself in, deeper, up, back, and she rides him like a small child at the park, rides and rides, her head thrown back, her eyes rolled back, dead. She looks down, the way he taught her to look, and sees them pressed together, hair both smooth and wiry: his is black and silver; hers, brown mixed with red and blonde.

His penis is so big and hard it curves. He catches her looking and when he calls attention to it, she blushes and he laughs. But how can she not watch? It is the best trick he has.

He pulls her down to the edge of the bed so her legs hang over the side and he opens her legs, lifts her ass with both his hands, each holding up one cheek, and she lifts her back, arches it, and he finds her furry mouth with his smooth one, his tongue.

He whispers in her ear, "Hold tight, baby, we're going to roll over now," but by then she needs to hear nothing, can hear nothing. She knows when he presses into her, the way his shoulders move against her, that they are rolling. He protects her head with his cupped hand. Then he is above her, sinking into her, then moving in and out.

This is the dream life, a life she had only dreamed, but without the details that one can glean only from experience. Their life is about nothing but intimacy, they have no public life. Their entire history has taken place in some tiny isolated space: the front seat of his car, this carriage house on the Lake, the bathtub, the bed. Sometimes when his back bothers him, they lie on the floor in the bedroom, stretched out, fully clothed; she lies on top of him, they don't talk. She knows these moments are numbered, that their lives will transfer to the big world very soon now, and she wants to remember—oh, God, she won't forget—what it is like to be in love like this at this late moment in a life.

She calls him darling, she calls him Robert. He says Bobby is his Bakersfield name. He tells her to call him Daddy and it is as if he has struck her. She is breathless with his knowledge of her, threatened by it, so she doesn't dare call him that for weeks until one night she rides high on him, the rain pounding the skylight above his bed, and she can't stand it and whispers for permission.

She calls him *Signor Parigi* or *Papa Parigi or Dottore Parigi* because he told her once in a hotel in Italy they thought his name was Paris, Robert Paris, and they called him *Signor Parigi*. They speak in broken English to each other. She buys him a little book at Rizzoli with a flat blue cover. Inside it explains: *il cazzo*–the cock, *la fica*–pussy.

She understands everything now, she is completely aware. He has taught her everything: he taught her to look, to watch his face and see the pleasure she was giving him. The pleasure a woman gives a man, she never understood before. The scales fall from her eyes like in fairy tales or the lives of her precious saints; knowledge is hers at last. At this advanced age, she becomes a woman. She can only pray, as women have before her, that he will be kind.

Some nights she leaves early to return to the small apartment she rented the day after she left her husband; she needs to walk her dog. When she gets there she calls him immediately.

"*Allo?*"

"*Signor Parigi?*"

"*Si.*"

"This is Baby. I am in my *casa* with my little . . . *carne, si? Carne* is dog?"

"She is a big dog, baby," he laughs.

"*Si.*"

She tells him to look out at the sky. "No, behind you," she says. "Look out near the garage."

There are flashes, quick shots of lightning, so the whole sky is lighted like one of those spotlights at a Hollywood premiere or used car dealer's lot when she was a little girl. "The sky is about to crack," she tells him.

He loves storms. As a little boy growing up in the San Joaquin Valley, he loved the sound of rain. He would hide under a tarp or put the metal top of a garbage can over his head, so the sound would be amplified, reverberate, echo more. He looked to weather the way she sat in the public library in Brookline, Massachusetts, the light filtering through the dusty high windows, searching for a way out of childhood in the books she read over and over.

"I want to teach you about weather," he says, "to be sensitive to changes in it."

He shows her how she can tell the direction of the wind by tossing dirt into it, or licking a finger and holding it up. He says you can tell the weather by the cloud formations: fair weather, cumulus, storm clouds. An Indian guide on a fishing trip in Canada showed him how the wind blowing the leaves inside out indicated rain. "One day, maybe two." They come out of a restaurant to see the moon round and red. "Blood on the moon, baby."

Sometimes in the middle of the night, she awakens and throws her camel's hair coat over her gown and goes out into the world, drives the short distance to his place to return to his warmth, his bed, so she can wake up with him.

They make a trip south to Virginia, the Chesapeake, Washington, DC. It is astonishingly easy for them to be together all the time. He drives his big car leisurely, with pleasure; he calls her Black Beauty. Cars are always female he tells her and he talks about the cars he has owned over the years, their spoke wheels and leather seats and powerful engines, as if they are women.

He tells her he hoped she would unbutton his jeans while he is driving and put her head in his lap and suck his cock, and when she obliges, he whistles, laughs, waves to the drivers who pass them on the left. They stop at roadside stands and buy jars of thick honey, jams, pickled watermelon rinds and tiny corns. The hand-written labels smudge, blur. They will never eat any of these things or remember to give them away.

He orders for her in restaurants. "You might like those soft shell crabs, love," he says, or the mousse cake or the avocado stuffed with something especially rich. He refers to her as his wife—she still wears the thin gold band from her marriage.

They stay in small inns, making love in the afternoon in small painted rooms with ceiling fans and chintz linens on the narrow iron beds and wicker armchairs and hooks for their clothes. They take baths in old tubs with brass fixtures. He smokes a cigar in the bath and scrubs her back seriously with a wash rag. He tells her she has the back of a little girl. "Do you know that, a child's precious back."

They lie in each other's arms on a plaid blanket in the sun in a field in Gettysburg where all those young men gave up their lives; he looks carefully for the names of his ancestors who fought for the Lost Cause of the South. At Monticello, he tells the ticket taker, "One senior and one adult. My daughter will pay you," and rushes ahead, imitating the swinging gait of a woman in front of them, hip upon hip, so that she howls with laughter and wets her pants and he has to loan her his handkerchief. He is always loaning her his handkerchief.

In Annapolis, the thickly air-conditioned room in an historic inn has a three-way mirror—a triptych of desire—across from the bed. He places her so she can see, puts a pillow to cushion her arms and head, lifts her hips high so she can watch him enter her from behind. But she cannot watch, blushes, turns her head; although she has said she always wanted to.

That night, he tells her how it feels to make love to her. He sits in a stuffed armchair near the window smoking while she lies in bed with a book in her lap, her reading glasses on, as he describes slowly, quietly, exactly how it feels: when he is on top of her, when she is on top of him, when he enters from behind, when he is in her mouth, and the angles of it: more forward, more back, above, on the side.

"But, baby," he says, "that's what it's about, the angle, right? Changing the angle?"

He seems surprised she doesn't know this, but how would she and how did he learn it?

He shrugs, laughs out loud. "Trial and error, I just tried it out."

He tells her about the first woman he had, a whore in Bakersfield. He was 13 years old, the littlest kid in a car full of boys out for an adventure. They dared him.

"I was scared . . . this old hotel. . . ." And he puts his head back and laughs. "I think it's been torn down. She was kind. She looked at me, saw what a skinny little kid I was and she was kind. Took off her clothes so I could touch her breasts. Took my little thing in her hand. . . . God, it felt good."

Then the next year, he had his first real girl friend. She was two years older; she sucked his cock. A nice girl, he says, a plain girl, she played the piano. He thinks she went to UCLA. "Patsy Lee Searles," he says, content.

A woman in the last moments of her attractiveness. I will never be this beautiful again, she thinks sadly, but with a kind of fierce pride that she recognizes it—at last, in this last moment, she feels free to admit how beautiful she must have been. A man in the last minute of youth, vitality, passion, the last time he will ever feel this way about a woman in his life.

Another room: a wicker chair, a handsewn quilt on the bed, the rotating ceiling fan, a table that holds scratchy covered books and an old atlas, her camera, a cast iron tub on a broad pedestal with French shower attachments—*allo, allo*. The formal parlor outside their door leads to the Italianate porch. It curves there, the screen doesn't quite shut, but the small swell offers privacy, two elaborate iron chairs and a table. And below the porch, the long slope of lawn and the beautiful old houses and chimneys of Staunton; church towers. Beyond those are the Blue Ridge Mountains, and twin peaks, round soft peaks called Bessie

Belle and Mary Gray, womanly peaks. The transom is etched with two roses.

As a child, her father had told her how animals protected themselves by taking on offensive or dangerous attributes: spikes and quills, poisonous skins and putrid odors. This she translated to the lives of her saints and fairy tale heroines: their beards and ass skins, wooden hands—how to protect your soul by not revealing your beauty. She had never grown into the slightly exotic, sexy woman she really was. Instead she learned to be shy, restricted, inhibited, studious.

How strange to be free to be this now. It is 3:30 in the morning. Suzanne sits in a pair of white silk pajamas and red slippers of woven leather, very fine with tassels. In the next room, asleep in the narrow bed is a man she barely knew last year at this time. This fact thrills her: the possibilities, the passion.

When they walk down the street at night, she watches their shadow selves: he is so tall above her, he drapes his arm casually around her shoulders, she has to reach up to touch him. He is guiding her—that is what she feels in bed with him—he is a strong gentle guide to her own wicked pleasure, wicked only in the sense that her desire for him is so deep it is insatiable.

On the sloped writing desk in the corner, a

Bible is opened to the 23rd Psalm: "The Lord is my Shepherd, I shall not want."

PART III

9

Summer in the country. In July, Suzanne leaves the city where she spent her entire adult life and heads north, following water—streams and lakes and bridges—and comes to live on a river for the reasons others have before, those of continuity, peace, momentum, the Protean elements of time and space. For the price extracted by society—her loss of a name, her status, her place in a small, protected society, most of her worldly goods—she is free to live with the man she had met in her dreams over the years, but whom she has known, after all, for a very short time.

During a wet romantic week-end she buys a small farmhouse, more than a hundred years old—and that is old around here—tucked into a valley, surrounded by blowsy fields and an exhausted apple orchard. A murky pond squats in a corner of the property. There is a sagging porch surrounding the little house, and, downstairs, a narrow kitchen with the curved appliances of the early Fifties, a main room with an old wood stove, another room that is soon filled with Amy's piano. Upstairs are two small bedrooms and an old-fashioned bath, and on the third floor, an attic where the workers bunked two to a narrow bed in haying season. The stairs are so steep and worn Lucia cannot climb them, although she tries and slips badly, tumbling down the last few before she gives up. She lies at the bottom and howls until Suzanne obediently descends to sleep with her old baby.

"You're ruining my sex life," she whispers irritably, pulling a mohair throw over her thin cotton gown. Lucia sighs and shudders, triumphant. And then, when the dog is lost in sleep, wheezing and snoring, Suzanne steals away, returns to the man in her bed, fitting her body against his, rousing him enough to wind a long arm around her and murmur dirty promises into her hair, damp and fragrant with summer.

Few of her things fit into this house, none of her share of the huge skeletal pieces of contemporary furniture with names from the great design movements of the early twentieth century, names that at one time excited her: Wiener Workstette, Bauhaus, Le Corbu, the Barcelona exhibition of 1929. The queen size mattress does not make it up the narrow staircase and must be exchanged for a double—the men who deliver it

116

drip sweat from their hands and armpits and chests onto the plastic cover as they lug it, cursing, up the stairs. Robert brings some antique pieces from his office; they buy kitchen chairs at auction, a curved glass-fronted cabinet for china; she lights tall candles and sticks them in old Mason jars found on the cellar steps.

Never in her life has she lived in this way. It seems to be part of a past that is not even hers. Maybe it belongs to Robert or to this region, but not to the ersatz-European salon existence that must be essentially hers. But, somehow, it is familiar. She remembers how she loved the illustrations of the pioneer women in her history books: wide eyed, their worn, pale faces peeking from the poke of a bonnet, their straight spines and long rounded arms. They reminded her of the dancers she had seen in Martha Graham's *Appalachian Spring*, a ballet she loved. So maybe this is her heritage, too. She suddenly knows what to do: stringing poles for tomatoes, picking wild berries in a big brimmed straw hat, washing dishes by hand, standing barefoot on the worn linoleum floor. Begin again, she whispers to herself.

The pump breaks, the basement fills with water, a massive limb of the ancient sugar maple snaps the first morning Robert is there, shaving upstairs, and puts a hole in the slate roof. The temperature rises, the humidity reaches the top and exhaustion sets in; she finds herself falling asleep downstairs on an old sofa with the dog. The plumbers replacing the rusting pump, the painters, the tree cutters, all looking for her, for money, signatures, directions, find her in torn jeans and a man's undershirt, asleep. They tiptoe around her sleeping form as tenderly as the Seven Dwarfs around Snow White. She seems to be under a spell.

Boxes stay stacked and packed in the apple barn. Her beloved books warp in the heavy summer humidity, her kitchen flatware is lost, so they use silver every day. She runs around with the hundreds of pieces of her former life in her hands—photos of her children, the small carved animals she put on her long dining table on holidays, crystal decanters and wine goblets, silver trays and pitchers, damask cloths and napkins (succinctly monogrammed)—looking for a place for them in her new life. There is none. She should have given Barry everything, she realizes now, it all belonged to him anyway, to his life.

Her children are confused, but they possess a stoicism she would not have thought belonged to them, until she remembers her own years of silent punishment. They have plans that preclude her, they are avoiding her: Josh is working for an attorney in the Justice Department in Washington, Amy travels with backpack and a Eurail pass and an old friend from high school.

Josh is angry with her, sometimes cold, impatient; sometimes she can barely speak through her tears to him. He is the only one she breaks down in front of—her son, her first born. Amy is easier, her problems with her father make her an ally of a kind. She sleeps twenty to a room in Czech, Dutch, German hostels; sends post-cards of native dancers and beer gardens; portraits of the Virgin; the precious, secular scenes of Dutch bourgeois life. Suzanne is touched by this recognition of her profession, but suddenly it is of no importance, it is strange to her now, to her life here. She sticks them guiltily in the peeling window frame next to her bed after barely reading them.

Sometimes her energy is vivid, intense, she feels free, brave, she divides her time between the house and her apartment in Evanston, where she has a month to go on her lease. She takes an exercise class, meets friends for lunch, drinks espresso in a coffee house she loves, eats dinner with Robert in small, obscure restaurants.

Several times she meets with her lawyer, a firm, gentle woman who is absolutely in charge of things. In the lawyer's mind this divorce is easy: the children out of the house, their educational funds in trust, a husband who wants to move to the opposite coast as soon as he can, a handsome lake front property that was quickly sold at an inflated price. The proceeds were immediately divided so they each could buy a house and take advantage of the roll-over. She almost congratulated Suzanne the first time she met her on her style, her timing, a situation perfectly organized for a civilized mid-life divorce. A court date has been set for the fall.

She is grateful her divorce is so easy, because it leaves her weepy, exhausted, anxious, flat. Suzanne returns home each time with the deep gratitude of a released prisoner, a patient, each mile she brightens, eases. When she crosses the narrow suspension bridge, she is happy again.

She buys up the last scrawny flats of geraniums from a farm stand and puts them into the large Italianate urns that once embraced the front door of her big house. She scrubs down a table from the early, student days of her marriage with turpentine and bleach, paints it the apple green of the farmhouse kitchen. Next year, they will have a serious garden, she tells Robert: herbs, lettuces. She will pull out these tall weeds and plant beds of bulbs, crocuses, daffs, tulips, iris, lilies, each one blooming when the others die, so that they are never without color and fragrance. She has never grown anything, put anything up or by, sewed curtains, painted old mirrors and picture frames these Matisse colors, worn her hair this way.

In the morning, when she takes a walk with the reluctant Lucia, the sun is just coming up over the river and the opposite shore is barely visible. Many mornings there is fog or mist lying over the valley like a old linen sheet or the scrim on a stage. This is when she sees the doe and her fawn or the heron whose nest is in the first clearing. One morning she spots an owl, his head screwed backwards, his face a cartoon-like mask. As if he has forgotten the time, he shakes himself suddenly and takes off, spreading the long and graceful wings that belie his chunky body.

Remembering Thoreau's requirements of the writer, that she give a simple and sincere account of her own life as if she were writing from a distant land, Suzanne sends a short note to her friend, Abby. Reading it, she is amazed to discover it is all about the natural world. On the bottom she scribbles: "Why am I telling you this? Fifteen years ago I spotted Jackie O. eating an ice cream cone on Cape Cod. If anyone asks about me, tell them this is how far I've traveled."

On week-ends, she and Robert lie on the porch furniture from her former manse, from that wide side veranda the real estate women coveted. She has painted it the new green. They discuss rumors around town—town topics, he calls them—the various theories and agendas others have for them. Suzanne has learned through a friend that an eminent classicist at the university announced at a dinner party that the cause of Suzanne's strange behavior—this means leaving a prominent husband of twenty-five years, a man not unlike the classicist himself—was her hysterectomy last fall. She has simply lost her mind. He reminds the assembled guests the origin of the Greek word for womb—hysteria—and how the ancients believed it wandered from organ to organ creating havoc as it went. Another friend reports that this year's writer in residence, a novelist famous for her swollen violent tales of unrequited love, has constructed an entire plot around Suzanne. She will set it in the latter half of the nineteenth century in the Catskills.

A woman who works at Robert's bank is overheard in the elevator comparing him to a rent-controlled apartment: the best ones are snapped up before they go on the market. No one bothers to worry about Barry who is, after all, a fully employed, ambulatory, heterosexual male, or any of the children, who are supposed to be grown. A few discuss the fate of her old dog Lucia; several mourn the wonderful parties Suzanne and Barry gave—all that good wine. People with bad marriages tend to be critical, punitive; people with good marriage are quieter, superstitious, you can almost hear them tossing salt or spitting into the wind.

Farther up the North Shore, tongues wag prodigiously, imaginatively: Louise has a curse put on Suzanne via her answering machine. Ominous organ music swells in the background; there is some sharp hissing and a throaty female voice warns that "They know, they know."

Louise sends over the maid to clean Robert's rental and to see what she can find. All she finds is a half-empty bottle of Chanel No. 19, the lacy bustier, a tortoise shell comb, a toothbrush, the book of Italian phrases, two ticket stubs for the ballet (a rare one: Balanchine's *Davids-bundlertanze*) and a volume of Neruda's *100 Love Poems*. Perhaps on the basis of this, Suzanne is described by his wife to her friends and children and anyone who will listen—and who can refuse such scandal in this veritable desert of respectability?—as unstable, intellectual, left-wing, neurotic, an *artiste*, a bohemian. Why not a circus performer? Suzanne wonders. It makes her think of Colette and for the first time she really understands *La Vagabonde* and all the other gutsy, fragile heroines of Colette's.

Louise refers to Suzanne as Robert's 'little friend,' and says they are living in la-la land. But she is not worried, she informs her daughters, he will be back as soon as he is tired of all that sex.

"And when will that be?" Suzanne asks.

Robert laughs. He lights his cigar and points out the summer constellations and cloud formations to her. He tells her that in 1812 a Frenchman gave names to the clouds: cumulus, cirrus, stratus and nimbus. For Christmas, he is planning to give her a brass telescope, slender, collapsible, antique. Suzanne remembers looking out on the night sky on the Lake last winter and longing for him. Lucia sleeps, her wizened head, her muzzle thin as the skull of a fox, peppered white, cradled in her own paws.

Suzanne listens to Robert's voice, lulled as if he is singing to her. His mother has sent his Granny's harmonica. It comes in the original worn blue Moroccan leather case. He traces its raised letters—Hoener, made in Germany, a faraway place he remembers looking up on the dusty globe in a library corner at school. A faded fan of directions for a few tunes is stuffed inside.

He thinks of Granny, her rocking chair leaning against the wall, her head thrown, back her tiny feet up on the porch rail—she gave him a nickel if he rubbed them. He blows into it, the sound is surprisingly sweet.

"What did she play?" Suzanne asks.

"*The Old Rugged Cross*," he smiles.

She requests *Home on the Range*.

In bed, in his arms, she longs for these moments as if they were already past. It seems like childhood, it is that pure, that temporary.

On Monday, Robert is gone. A month ago he traded in his Mercedes for a Chevy pick-up, to the amazement, the dismay and chagrin of his daughters. Nell is simply aghast. Is he planning to come into the city in that truck? God, don't park it in front of her place. Couldn't he use that on the week-ends? But that is the point, he explains patiently. How can he relay to this urban child the pleasure of stepping out of the truck in his parking garage downtown each morning, patting it fondly on the tailgate like the rump of a horse.

"Take good care of her, Willie," he says to the man who runs the parking garage.

"I will, Mr. Parrish," Willie promises.

Has Willie heard the rumors, the stories about this gentle, polite man who has always treated him with friendship and respect, tipped him generously at Christmas; has he always known with the instincts men have about each other, that there was another side to Robert, the proverbial man caught inside a suit. There seems to be a current of understanding between them, a familiarity: former soldiers, comrades, men.

In the meantime, Robert is courting his daughters. They meet him for dinner in the city, a trio of handsome blonde women, well-groomed and dressed in the tailored clothes of a more formal time with fat gold earrings and bracelets and tasseled pumps. They are surprised and dismayed by the chain of events; they are out-spoken. Nell cries the most, while Anne cross-examines him.

"You'd better start telling us about Suzanne," she says, "because right now all we know is what Mother tells us and we hate her. That, and that she wears Chanel 19," she adds slyly.

He seems stunned to learn what their mother has said; he is surprised even more by his own children's narrow views. Why did he expect them to accept this so easily? Did he think it was because they had witnessed his cold, loveless marriage or had he thought they loved him more than their mother? Can his daughters be so selfish?

He holds the hand of the youngest, Margaret.

She is home from boarding school briefly, before she goes off on a French exchange summer and is flattered to be included. She rolls her eyes, agrees with one or the other of her sisters or says nothing and lets each of them pet her, stroke her long hair. He orders them vodka martinis with twists and huge charcoal steaks and thick tomato and onion salads.

Soon they begin to relax and become the jokey girls he knows. They hang onto his hands and call him Daddy and kiss him on the mouth and then the cheek; they love him and cannot live without him. How could he leave them? But he has not left them, he says, amazed, he has left their mother. They know how she is, he says, but they are deaf to reason. Oh, how they miss him.

Sometimes he visits Louise to pick up his mail or a kitchen object he would like to use and rarely is allowed to take. He tries to discuss medical insurance, finances; he is teaching her how to keep a checkbook. When he walks up the wide steps of his house, his heart feels as if there is a stone hanging from it, his heart heavy with the burden of guilt.

Once, when Louise was visiting her sister in Florida, he took Suzanne to see it. "I want you to see where I was kept a prisoner," he said.

Suzanne was overwhelmed by its order, its

decoration; it looked like the glossy photographs of homes in a slick magazine, it was that static. "How could you have lived here?" she asked him. When he could not answer, she told him about a great house in France where they had to deposit their shoes at the entrance and skate carefully across the wide parquet floors on modified pot holders so their dirt would not touch the precious woods.

How could he have lived here; now he sees. It is a museum, each piece in place, polished, shined, the Doulton figurines in their familiar places, family photographs in ornate silver or gilt frames, thick silk tassels holding back the heavy damask drapes, the brocade pillows stiffly arranged on sofa backs. One pillow, embroidered in bargello by Louise, reminds him that "You cannot be too thin or too rich."

Nothing has changed in his absence; she could have replaced him with a large stuffed dummy seated in his leather wing chair in the library. He wonders whether it matters to Louise if he is here or not. He cannot remember the last time she told him she loved him and he guesses she does not.

But had she ever? She must have felt something to get into bed with him, but then their sex life was never very good, even in the beginning, even when he was excited, thrilled, frankly, by his love for her. Had she loved the pink cheeked, hairless young man who spurned her, rebounding her into his grateful arms? Years later when they met him at a party at the country club, he could barely drag her away, she was so drunk, and she clung to the blazered arm of her former beau, bald now, still boyish. Robert remembers he had a cigarette holder, an odd accouterment, a prop. Foppish, that was it, he thinks, a foppish man, soft, a bit feminine.

Bringing iced tea out to the screened-in porch, Louise is, as always, chatty, perky, flirty. She looks as if she just stepped out of a bandbox—a favorite expression of her mother's—she is little girl dressed for a birthday party. She seems like a child to him now, another daughter. Perhaps, if he had treated her like one, she would have liked him more. She seems not to have noticed anything has changed. He feels like the headmaster talking with one of his particularly recalcitrant students who doesn't understand he is telling her that she is flunking out of school.

She simply refuses to discuss anything, or see a lawyer. He will be back, she says airily to her friends, her daughters, her shrink. She has it on the best authority: someone very wise and mysterious and not of this world has told her that.

She gives Robert the same cheek to peck he used to, and waves gaily from the double front doors as if he were going off to work and will be home that evening for dinner, as usual.

When he is gone, Suzanne sits in his big leather chair, sleeps in the tops of his pajamas, paints her toenails the pinky-orange of teen-aged summers, sleeps on the sofa with Lucia at her feet. She cooks pasta every night—penne—tossing it with tomatoes and fresh basil, olive oil and cheese and eats it with her fingers while she watches videos of French films she loved when she was a student: *Jules et Jim*, *The 400 Blows*, Renoir's *Rules of the Game*. Before he returns, she shaves her legs carefully, up to the crotch, trims her pubic hair with his nail scissors, washes her long hair with new shampoo, waits for him at the gate, listening for the sound of his high tires on the narrow gravel road.

Their summer life: tomatoes and corn and fragrant soft melons, meats cooked on the grill. Frank Sinatra plays through the open windows, and Robert in one of his long starched aprons dances her around the shaky porch.

"Restless," he tells her, "I have been restless all my life."

He loved Hemingway when he was a youth,

read his books over and over. He believed that life would be his, a big life with travel and wars and the admiration of tough men and the love of beautiful, ultimately unattainable women, booze and danger. But not many of us get to live that life.

He speaks again and again of a wasted life, a life that wasn't his, hadn't belonged to him, but to the others: Louise, his children, his career, but Suzanne refuses to see it that way. All lives are merely preparation for the real life, she says, the one of spirit and imagination, an inner life. She believes they had to pass through these things, travel each of these stations like pilgrims, so when they came together, they would know it for what it was. Before, it was all a test, a trial.

She takes his hands when he talks like this, holds them, rubs them, places them on her eyes, her breasts, but he isn't moved. He is lost to her, somewhere else. She blows hot breath into his ear, puts her mouth on his neck, shoulder, licks him slowly. She tells him now he will have that life, she will save him as he has saved her. Finally, he smiles wearily, as if she is a very small child who understands nothing.

Our life in the country, he calls it other times, our lucky life, and awakens cheered, talks about taking his grandsons down the river in old inner tubes, getting a big yellow dog to ride in the back of his pick-up, raising chickens. He will call his rooster Charlamagne, name the hens after favorite Paris restaurants: Benoit, L'ami Louis, Allard. They will give a Christmas party and invite only the neighbors; he describes meat smoking in a covered pit, black-eyed peas cooking in the Dutch oven that belonged to his Granny.

They pick raspberries and blackberries in the woods and he bakes cobbler for her in a blackened iron skillet. He finds an old ice-cream maker in the barn and churns out chewy thick vanilla to eat with it. In the mornings there are pancakes and biscuits, slab bacon from a local butcher who smokes his own. She is getting fat.

There is a small store down the road where she gets the mail. It sells everything from baskets to incense sticks, New Age handbooks on healing, T-shirts, milk and soda pop. Robert meets everyone; soon he can greet everyone by name, his big arm outstretched to shake hands or pat backs. On the mornings he is there, he can be found drinking coffee with the locals who are fond of arguing politics and reading the Chicago papers and *The Progressive* from Madison, before they head off to tile floors and build bookcases for the city folks moving closer and closer.

Some mornings, she looks up at the ceiling beams where he hung his skillets and copper pots and braids of garlic and and chili peppers, and notices he added a long Italian salami or the stiff octagonal box of a Christmas pannetone, or a straw hat with a choke of silk violets he bought on Michigan Avenue for her.

In the evenings they take a walk along the river. A narrow tow-path had been carved out of the woods for horses and mules many years ago, before the railroads came this far north. They have to climb down a steep bank to get to it. One night Robert stops in pain, he can't catch his breath.

"Wait," he says, "honey, stop."

She scrambles back, alarmed, his face is gray, sweaty. "Are you all right?" she asks stupidly.

He raises a hand, shakes his head. "Whew. I don't know what happened. I couldn't catch my breath."

"Has that happened before?"

"A few times," he admitted. "Last week in the parking garage."

"Why didn't you tell me?"

"Oh, honey, you're not going to be one of those women. . . . Don't get excited. I've told you I had that old problem with hypoglycemia when I'm under a lot of stress."

"Have you ever had any trouble with your heart?"

"Heart's fine." He straightens up, grabs one of

her wrists with a hand.

"Maybe you should. . . ."

"Please, baby," he says, coaxing her with his hands.

"You look better," she says relieved, leaning back against him.

"Honey," he says to her. "I hope I die an old man in your arms in this house, but if not, remember, we had to do this."

10

In September, she is divorced; she comes in from the country. It is a time of the year she thinks of as the beginning of the year, her life having always been ordered by the academic calendar. It is Indian summer, a name she has always liked, although she does not know what it means or if it refers to the colors or the weather or has anything to do with Indians at all.

Barry flies in from California for the day. She picks him up at O'Hare. They brush against each other awkwardly, apologetically; they are extremely polite. She offers him the Barcelona chairs. He seems surprised: she had fought for them only a few months before. He tells her how well the old library table looks in his dining room. He asks how Lucia is making the adjustment to country life. He confides problems with a woman he is seeing, an attorney, a number of years younger than he, but he is boasting, too. They are suddenly time travelers together, commuters in a new age; it is all as natural and as strange as can be.

She wears the black dress she wore during that long winter of funerals. But it is not death she is reminded of this morning, it is her wedding: the legality, the solemnity, the ritual, Barry in a dark suit and black shoes, the litany of names, signatures, questions asked and answered. She remembers how, her own mother dead, it was his mother who took her to look for a dress and, when some adjustments had been made, she had pivoted slowly on a circular velvet platform in front of the triple mirror in the Bridal Salon at Filene's to see—who was that pale, pretty, young woman surrounded by white tulle and pearls? She remembers going for their blood tests so early in the morning it was still dark. Because she was afraid, Barry had scheduled them without telling her. They went to her father's office at 5:30 AM, where his nurse met them—her odd wedding gift. She is still thinking of this when the proceedings are over, so she crosses the aisle of the small courtroom, the grooms's side, and gives Barry a kiss to the discomfort of their lawyers.

"You may kiss the bride," she says aloud.

Sometimes she will be struck with a wave of longing for her old life, for her house, the order of the high-ceilinged rooms, the predictability of a life lived a certain way forever, for the long hours without interruption in her book lined study, sometimes even for Barry's lack of attention, which allowed her to day-dream. She thinks she would give almost anything for it to be twenty years ago, the first day of school, a long pan of brownies cooling on a kitchen counter, while she waited eagerly for the sounds of bikes in the gravel driveway and that sweet cry: "Mom, I'm home!" They would sit and talk and tell her a million things until, as abruptly, they were gone again. It had taken almost thirty years to create that life, losing it was sadder than she could have ever guessed.

As Barry had predicted back in Berkeley, she is denied tenure at the college where she had taught for six years. They offer her a one-year contract, but the commute would be too long. It isn't worth it, she reasons; she will use the time to finish her book.

Poems come to her the way they did in adolescence; all that nature imposing itself, she suspects, the way the impetus was once emotion. Maybe she will write stories, she has always wanted to write or paint for that matter, or maybe give ballet classes: that is how she is these days. She watches the dwindling sums in her bank statements—the repairs to the house have been more expensive than she thought. Even with the generous settlement she received—they had accumulated more money than she would have imagined—she cannot live more than a few years without some other income.

She is frequently alone in the country and, without a reason to go into Chicago, she doesn't go very often—just to have her teeth cleaned, buy serious shoes, books and foreign magazines, good coffee beans, look at some paintings or photographs. Friends from her former life still call, some of them make the trip out and spend the night. They exclaim over the landscape, the pretty old house; some are envious of her having a wonderful new love, but they rarely come again.

Everyone wants to know how her work is going: isn't it wonderful she has full-time to concentrate on her book, is she happy at last? Her children are interested, too, and worried, she knows, about her financial situation. She laughs and tells them a book won't make any difference. She sets up her computer in the tiny room with Amy's piano, on an old table with a sewing machine base she found at a barn sale. Lucia curls up happily under it, so she has no room for her feet; she straddles one of the rickety kitchen chairs. She has a proper desk chair, high backed with rolling coasters and a big wooden desk rotting away in the barn, but it won't fit through the door to the house.

She begins to need things she cannot find, she begins to want things she does not own anymore: the tall goblets from a Silver Oak tasting, the Oxford Dictionary, a slotted spoon, Barry's field coat. Needing a book for a review she had agreed to do for the journal Monique edits, she is filled with such longing to just see it—the friendly purple and yellow jacket, the quirky angular illustration, the collage of photographs—she rushes out to the apple barn. She knows exactly where it sat for years on a broad white shelf of the copious bookcases in the dining room of her house on the Lake.

All her passions—Colette, Bloomsbury, Paris in the Twenties, Frieda Kahlo, books of photographs by Lisette Model and Berenice Abbott, thick books of Giotto's paintings and Piero's—are in these boxes; suddenly, she must have them. She confronts the sixty cartons of books stacked to the rafters. She can barely lift them, but manages to push them off each other. With one of Robert's knives, she slashes open the boxes, one after another, pulls books out randomly. There must have been a leak, the floor, the walls are damp. Book after book is molded, warped, water soaked, ruined.

She finds books from college, books of her mother's—the biographies of the heroes of her

mother's radical youth, her love of the ballet,
scrapbooks she made of the 1933 World's Fair,
all the mother-dreams Suzanne inherited and re-
pressed and fought and now treasures. She begins
to weep, great heaving sobs. Her children's books
are damaged, too: *Winnie the Pooh* and Maurice
Sendak, the *Purple and Red and Yellow Fairy Tales*,
Amy's horse books and lonely teenager books,
Josh's sports heroes.

For the first time she sees what her children,
her friends knew about her and feared, that she
had always lived through books, that she has little
idea of how to put together a life. There are too
many books, there is nothing she can do, so she
quickly dumps them back into the boxes, ruining
them for certain now, and covers them and flees.

The next day, she feels stronger, surer of herself; she carries the twenty-four volumes of the
encyclopedia into the house, laying them out on
tables, chairs, the stairs. She wipes the backs and
front as if they are her own children's fevered faces,
and leaves them to dry. This is a rescue mission.
So much has perished and now she must save
the last pieces of her lost life before she is completely alone.

The holidays loom. Robert ticks them off happily: Halloween, Thanksgiving, then the best of

all, he loves Christmas, he says. Suzanne stares at him in disbelief. She has never known anyone over the age of ten or so, who still loves Christmas. But, of course, he is so different than anyone she knows, maybe he does love it, maybe he knows something about it she does not and will teach her. He talks about standing rib roasts and Yorkshire pudding, he mentions candy corn and pumpkins, cornbread and oyster stuffing, the black eyed peas and ambrosia salad on New Year's Day, as if these missing children of theirs will appear magically, smiling and pleasant at the table. And what of the table? It seats six maybe, this relic of her Cambridge youth with the unmatched kitchen chairs. She cannot imagine Robert's elegant daughters and their hearty husbands perched on these. Although she knows they would be polite and patient, she would feel too much like the poor relation. And Josh has already made plans with his father, and maybe Amy will, too.

But other times, she feels happy. They place huge pots of yellow mums on the porch, a young man and his wife come to stack a cord of apple and oak logs against the far side of the house. Robert buys the biggest pumpkin he can find and says he will carve a jack-o-lantern with a wide mustache like the one he is planning to grow. She picks apples to make sauce and pies, she carries in pine cones and sticks for kindling, she collects nuts and puts them in an old wooden bowl. She is a squirrel, she is a keeper, she is a gatherer like the women she taught about.

There are things she had learned from her mother's grandmother, too. On Halloween, after they carved her jack-o'lantern, she learned to separate the plump white seeds from the orangy pulp and dry them on newspapers. The next day they baked them on cookie sheets bent and blackened with use and covered them with coarse salt to eat. Because of her, Suzanne imagines winter as pots of soup and fires and candles burning in the frosty windows. She remembers how they forced bulbs to bloom in the frigid Boston winter in chipped tea cups, the saucers balancing on banging radiators. The grandmother spoke of a Europe of featherbeds and wolves and wild berries.

Suzanne has always dreamed of a life of wide contrasts: a country life and a city life, Russian winters and tropical summers, weeks of hard work, wearing the same dreary clothes, struggling in the country and then the miracle of a week-end in the city with its shops and restaurants, the theatre, wearing perfume and beautiful dresses, long coats and high heeled shoes. In those days, she had imagined she would become a great woman, a remarkable woman of wide range and intelligence with a strong and rare beauty, if only she could free herself from ordinary life. Love had made her courageous, heady, spirited for a moment, but it is fleeting, the spell is breaking. It has been months since she has seriously worked or earned any money, been to the movies, worn dressy clothes or seen her children.

Planting bulbs along the river bank, she plunges her spade into a soft spot and exposes an active wasp's nest. She did not know they built down, not just up, tunneled far below the earth. They swarm, encircle her, nest in her hair; stinging her scalp, cheeks, neck, her forearms. She starts running, up the bank, the steps, her hands frantically searching her hair, shaking it loose from the hairpins, pulling off the old sweatshirt, a silk undershirt, screaming as she goes. Lucia barks weakly from the porch.

"Robert!" she cries. "Robert, help!"

But he is not there, he is gone, visiting Anne and his grandsons at their beach house in Michigan. She struggles to fill the sink with water and baking soda, her hands swell and go numb, she vomits, she leans hard against the counter and does not faint.

Later he calls her, says he has tried all morning and received no answer. "Oh, love," he says when she tells him about the wasps. "Oh, my little love, my darling girl. Are you all right?"

Now she is brave and funny. She tells him that she took an antihistamine right way and made a mash of baking soda and water to put on the bites, and bathed in vinegar to take way the sting. She looked it up in that old book she has about remedies. Of course, all they had was that very fine wine vinegar from France in the ceramic bottle so it was a twenty dollar bath. She listens for his laughter. She tells him that she called the drug store and the pharmacist asked if her lips and tongue were swollen and black, and when she said she had to get off the phone and look in the mirror, the pharmacist said he almost came out there right away, but of course, they weren't.

"Vespeds, that's what they're called. Isn't it a lovely name? Are you having a good time?" she asks. Now that she is assured of his love and concern, she can be big and generous.

"Oh, love," he says, and laughs, "this is really funny. I came into the guest room and it looked so familiar and then I realized that Louise had given Anne the drapes and spreads from my old room."

"I guess she knows you're not coming back," she says lightly. There is no answer, so she asks cautiously, "Do you mind being recycled?"

"No," he says finally, "I'm glad the children are getting something out of this."

But she can tell it makes him sad.

11

They begin to travel, foreign places with high beds and heavy linens, duvets and bed rolls, tall shuttered windows dusty with the thin afternoon sunlight of late autumn. Somehow it is easier for them to be here than at home alone together, a peculiarly nineteenth century solution. She thinks of the couples in *The Good Soldier*. "This is the saddest story I have ever heard," she says aloud.

"What, baby?"

"Oh, a line from a novel."

"Put your pearls on, honey," he says, "it'll make you feel better." They dress for dinner and go out into an urban evening.

They go to Paris. They stay in a hotel that is very old and small—on the Left Bank of course—a tiny room with a wide bed with a deep soft mattress that sags and the classic pillow roll and velvet hangings and a fat pouf of a chair, a hotel frequented over the century by famous and less famous writers. In the morning the maids bring crisp croissants, red jams shimmering like jewels, the many clattering pots of coffee and milk, wide mouthed cups, a paper napkin folded under. There are sugar cubes wrapped in papers that say: *Daddy*, *Began*. Girls from the country, slender with downy arms and an occasional gold tooth, they gain an education in an instant as they steal a blushing glance at the arrangement of the bed clothes.

Robert wants to see medieval Paris: the old university, the museum of Cluny, Notre Dame, the Ile, where Suzanne slept with her first lover. She wants to eat oysters, the wide icy platters balanced on their wire cages; she wants to walk the boulevards in the rain under one black umbrella. She wants to look at the paintings she remembers from her first time and can find in her sleep, tiny Dutch paintings hidden in the empty side rooms off the main galleries of the Louvre; these are still lives captured just the instant before death. Sometimes, too, at dusk, she sits weeping for no reason in their room as the yellow lights of the city come on.

"You are in your favorite city with the love of your life," Robert says. "Aren't you happy?"

Each journey recalls another journey: snapshot images of cafes, hotels, galleries, restaurants, the grand avenues. She sees the college girl, the young wife and mother, the art historian, as if her selfs are Russian dolls fitting tight within each other, each journey containing another journey and another one. Instead of moving forward, she feels sucked farther and farther back in her past. At night, she dreams the terrible dreams once again: her children are in an accident and call out for her, she dreams of Lucia, alone in the kennel. One night she dreams Barry is lying on a slab in the morgue and she must identify his body. His body is rigid and blue but his lips are still moving and one of his arms jerks. She tells the assembled they cannot bury him yet, he is not dead.

She sits waiting in a hotel lobby in Paris or Prague or Rome and counts up other hotel lobbies and wonders how she had begun this life at all, coming from a bleak middle-class childhood on a street with symmetrical brick houses where you looked out onto almost identical views from all the windows. All these places she had looked to as being the capitals of her soul, had longed for when she wasn't there.

When she was young, each trip, each time, she vowed to re-do her whole life: learn a new cuisine, conquer a language, dress in the mode of the women on the streets. She would buy something: a pen, a scarf, a fan, flat Moroccan slippers, or sabots. She would smoke Gauloise or Players or the wonderful black cigarettes from Dunhill, switch from coffee to tea to wine to aquavit. She would collect hundreds of post-cards from museums, write them idly in a cafe, send few. She, who had made art the focus of her life, now drives past whole fields of ancient temples, bronze warriors dug from the sea, museums full of frescoes and mosaics, without a twinge of longing or regret. "See Naples and die!" the Romantics of the nineteenth century had said. Well, Naples is 20 kilometers away and she does not bother.

In Ravello, after dinner, they wander into a walled garden across from their hotel.

"*Prago*," the old gardener says.

They follow him. Robert points out the fig trees. "I wonder if they are white figs or black—how do you say white—*blanco*, *bianco*, *negro*, *nero*?" Robert's California Spanish confuses him. "We had them with sugar and cream in the morning when I was a child. Did you used to, honey?"

She laughs: sugar and cream on figs? She was happy with an occasional banana. Robert splits one open with his big hands, parts it just enough to reveal its flesh—soft, pink, tapering; *la fica*, she remembers from the little blue book. She tells him the female wasp is trapped inside the fig while depositing her eggs. She must die, and wingless male children are born of this violent act. Does he know this?

The gardener slits one rose with his worn knife, presents it to her formally. See, she wants to say, men still find me attractive. She smiles at the waiters and tells Robert outrageous stories she has heard about waiters in southern countries who marry German countesses or are sent plane tickets by Swedish banking heiresses to get them through the long winters. She talks about waiters who flirted with her, wanted to take her dancing, offered to find baby sitters for her children so they could be alone with her.

While gracefully filleting their fish, one waiter tells them in the winter he works on a cruise ship in America, docked in Miami. She noticed the steel grey BMW with Florida plates parked in the lot next to the hotel. He flashes all his beautiful white teeth and sighs. "All the women," he says, bowing over their plates, "they want to take the Cruise of a Lifetime."

Robert becomes quieter and quieter, he is worn out, he misses his daughters, his routine. He is distracted by a shortage of money, the loss of honor, and an accompanying guilt. She asks him if he is well, he seems slow, his skin grey, almost pickled at times; their love making drops to below the national average. When they climb the steps of a cathedral or walk the streets of an old market town, he is quickly out of breath.

No, no, he waves his hand and distracts her with a coffee or a story. Every now and then he feels fine, puts on his beautiful cashmere coat and a wide silk tie, he lights a cigar and tells a story or sings a cowboy song and then makes love to her the way he did in the beginning. He is big and leisurely and loving, remembering everything, making up some things. He tells her he is a Roman candle or the Tower of Pisa or the Eiffel Tower, depending on the locale.

In Rome, they stay at the top of the Spanish Steps, not the Hassler. The Hassler is where he stayed with Louise, of course, and in the evening sometimes, he sits in the lobby and smokes his cigar and everyone says hello to him, not because they remember him from three years ago, but because he is the kind of man who belongs in that lobby. Yet he is happy with their hotel, astonished at how much less it costs and how comfortable it is. It has a roof garden, too, and they have drinks up there, *camparisoda* in tiny triangular bottles with a little dish of child-size ice cubes. Rome suits him, it has size and style. The flowers and climate remind him of southern California, the wine is good, the food is great, the women are beautiful. On fine days, you can sit outside and enjoy all three.

In Rome, she remembers that it is the anniversary of her mother's death: her mother has been dead more than thirty years and the flavor of it is as sharp in her mouth as it was then. She remembers how the phone rang in the middle of night and how she and her father sat in bathrobes, drinking tea, but she doesn't remember what they talked about, except that it wasn't death. Now she remembers only the sound of the telephone and her continued fear of it for years, how each time it rang it startled her with the certainty of bad news.

Never really strong, she is losing her nerve, she is falling, she is fading, she feels like a Jean Rhys heroine, down on her luck, wearing the kind of clothes that advertise one's despair and poverty. She looks in strange mirrors and the windows of shops and doesn't recognize herself—her hair, her clothes belong to another women; without exercise, her body is changing, rounding, thickening.

In Rome, she has her hair cut—always a mistake. Without her hair she is a little lost, she misses the gestures of putting it up and taking it down. At first the contrast itself was thrilling: the back of her neck, the exposure of her fine boned face, but soon it is curling in the damp autumn air, the highlights turning a terrible orangey blond. Instead of looking like a Roman countess, as hoped, she thinks she looks like someone's middle-aged aunt from Iowa. There appears to be no way to escape your life; maybe that is what is meant by destiny. It was Robert's desire for her that made her feel confident, beautiful, young, and without it she is again a pale, fading woman balancing precariously and alone on the edge of the rest of her life.

12

She goes to pick Lucia up at the kennel when they return from Rome and finds the woman who owns it waiting for her, weeping.

"I don't know what to do for her, Mrs. Miller, she can't walk, she won't eat. She just stares. I think she thought you weren't coming back for her and she wanted to die."

Suzanne comforts the woman although her heart is pounding. Together they go back to the cage where Lucia is sleeping on a stack of old blankets piled on her palette. For a minute, when Suzanne kneels down to talk to her, the dog opens her eyes and begins to whimper. She tries valiantly to get up, to lick Suzanne's face.

"I wouldn't leave you," Suzanne whispers, "I was coming back for you." Tears are running down her face now, too.

"You should put her down, Mrs. Miller, I've thought that for a long time now, but I couldn't get myself to tell you. She's too frail, she wets herself and dirties the place, and she can't move.

That's in her blood, you know, she was bred to run. You have to allow her some dignity."

Suzanne looks in Lucia's eyes. They have been faded with cataracts for several years, but now she can see they are almost opaque. "She's all I have . . . you know, from my other life, from when my children were small, when I. . . ."

She is crying so hard she can't stop. She wishes Robert were here with her. Where is he? At work, and then he is taking Nell and her husband to dinner. He wanted Suzanne to come, too, but his daughters still refuse to meet her. Suzanne resents them in almost the same instant as she understands and pities them.

She hears the kennel owner's voice again: "She thought you weren't coming back for her and she wanted to die." Again and again, she neglected this dog for Robert, his trips, his needs, not to mention her children. She has just been grateful they are busy, don't need her or want her. What choice would she make then? She remembers a week-end Josh came to visit and she could barely sit through an evening's conversation with her own son. All she wanted was to get into bed with Robert. And Amy? She had hustled her off to a three week language program before her regular classes started this fall.

"What should I do?" She strokes Lucia's head.

"I can call the vet," the woman says. "I'll tell him you're on your way."

They carry the dog to her car, placing her on a blanket in the back seat. On the way to the vet Suzanne sings to her, the medley she used to sing to her children: lullabyes, Joan Baez, a little Peter, Paul and Mary. She is back in her old neighborhood now, the place where she feels she lived her entire life. She has kept the vet she had brought Lucia to the morning she picked her up at the greyhound shelter, many years before. She talks soothingly to the old dog, who has fallen asleep again, but when they arrive at the vet, Suzanne breaks down again. He shakes his head and agrees there is nothing to do. He flexes one of Lucia's knee joints.

"Do you hear that?" he asks. "It's all gritty, she has nothing left in her joints."

"Is she in pain?"

"I'll give her something for that right now."

His assistant comes in with some forms; Suzanne's hand shakes as she signs them.

"I want her cremated and I want her ashes," she says firmly, realizing she has been thinking about this for a long time.

"That'll be another hundred dollars," the girl says.

"I don't care."

"If you'll just go in there," the vet says, lifting the dog.

Lucia suddenly rallies as he carries her out, cranes her head, looking around for Suzanne.

"I can't," Suzanne says, "I can't do this. Please, just take her."

"Do you want to say good-bye?" he calls to her.

She is in the parking lot by the time he finishes his question.

She drives to her old house and parks in front and weeps. She has failed Lucia, she is a coward, she could have provided some comfort at the end, but she knows she could not watch her die. She has let everyone down, a man who had taken her word in good faith for twenty-five years, her children, her friends, her own sense of self.

She never said good-bye to her mother. The last time she saw her mother was on a dreary November day. Impatient to get out of the hospital, get on with her life, she supposes, she waved hastily from the doorway after a short, perfunctory visit. She was fifteen. No one told her she would not see her mother again, that her mother wouldn't be in that hospital bed the following week or weeks following, that she wouldn't wait until Suzanne grew up enough to pay attention.

She had been sick as long as Suzanne had been an adolescent. She lay in a coma for days, but Suzanne had never gone back to see her. The day after the funeral she had insisted on going to school. Her father didn't know what to do with her. She would not talk about it, she would not weep.

When her father died she was in Stockholm and by the time she made it home, he was stretched out in his coffin in a shroud, his big nose hard and blue with death. She does not know how to say good-bye and she did not learn the old grandmother's trick for remembering by lighting candles in thick jars once a year.

She gets out of the car and walks up the gravel path to the front door. No one is home. The house had been bought by a young wealthy couple with no children, although they hoped to have them, the woman had told Suzanne shyly during an earlier visit. His parents bought the house for them. She walks around the yard for a few minutes, the leaves are bare, the lake is gray, shallow. Her marriage is dead, and the little family who lived in this house, and the dog who lived with this family.

Oddly, having Lucia's ashes make her feel better. She has been handed an elaborately decorated certificate where she is referred to as the loyal companion. She tucks the neat little cardboard box on a shelf in the bedroom closet and, when she needs to get a sweater or a different pocketbook, she looks at the box and imagines Lucia is sitting there waiting for her. She thinks the next time her children are home, or in the spring, they can bury the ashes somewhere on the property. But after a month, she takes the box back to the old house, and when she is sure no one is there, enters the yard and sprinkles the ashes carefully among the azalea bushes and shrubs.

Nature suddenly seems ominous: the first snows come. On her solitary walks she watches a deer struggling to find her way out of the woods, out of breath, panting, limping. A hawk, mistakenly shot by hunters, trails a long thin line of red on the frozen canal, flapping its wings courageously, until it is exhausted. A row of geese follows the floating dead body of a brother. The river has risen angrily, wiping out last year's nest of the heron. Storms come that flood the basement and barn—she has never fixed the roof. The power goes off for hours at a time. In an ice storm, she rams her old Volvo into a stone wall. Of course, she never had the windshield wipers fixed either.

Robert has a cold in his chest that will not go away. Finally, he schedules a doctor's appointment for Friday morning. After two minutes on the treadmill, the doctor tells him to stop, to sit down, put on his things and come down the hall to talk. By the time he gets out to the country to tell her, he has considered many things, made plans and arrangements, an appointment in the city the following week with a coronary specialist.

Sitting in his hospital room, fumbling with the open, unread pages of a book of Russian fairy tales, she watches him sleep. She has no claim, she has nothing: she doesn't have his name or his child or his ring, nothing. If he dies, his daughters will pull up in a big rental truck and remove it all: his big hat and the worn boots, his applewood walking stick and his cashmere shawl, his jazz, the few pieces of furniture from his office, his copper pots and cast iron skillets, his cookbooks, and the pocket watch his father set once a month with the clock at the railroad depot.

When she gets home, she runs upstairs and quickly feels into a drawer for a handkerchief and finds the worn smooth case of the harmonica. She comes across the navy v-necked sweater she had worn the first night she stayed with him. After making love, he had dressed her, gently pulling his pajamas bottoms over her bare trembling legs, dropping the sweater over her flushed face, the low neck exposing her breasts; one fell out. He tucked it back gently.

"Are you warm, love?" he asked. He cooked for her for the first time that night, some sauce made of scallions and parsley, garlic, oil and butter in a scratched Teflon sauté pan, the pasta boiled in a too small saucepan, the only pots in the place. How good it was, delicious. He stood in the rented kitchen in his travel robe, barefoot, young, lost, completely happy.

She loved to watch him cook, watch him chop things with precision, love, leisure, total absorption. This habit, his rare sensibility—the complete loss of real time—he gave to cooking, to making love, to watching nature. Once, early, waiting for the exercise class to begin, he had described the preparation of lamb chops for her, his hands making slow circular motions of oiling them, his fingers sprinkling imaginary garlic over them, then rubbing some more in.

"That's when I knew," she told him while he cooked that first meal.

"Knew what, love?"

"That you'd be great in bed."

He put his big head back and laughed.

So many scenes flood now. "Oh, god, don't die,"

she whispers to him.

When she finally meets them it is like seeing the film of a novel you have read many times, characters made flesh and blood, although not always the way you imagined. They are larger than she could have guessed, sleeker, well-groomed, less finely pretty, more friendly and open. They push past her to his hospital bed.

"Oh, Daddy," they cry aloud. Nell bursts into tears, Anne begins plumping his pillows and massaging his neck with great energy.

"We told Magsie not to come," Anne says. "I mean, we think that was right, don't you, Daddy? She's too young and she had a big date this weekend." She rolls her eyes.

Robert raises himself, looked past them to see Suzanne in the corner. "Honey?"

"I think I'll take a walk," she says wanly, then smiles. "Would anyone like me to bring them some coffee?"

They stare at her for a minute, as if they had forgotten she was there, and then they shake their heads. She wants desperately to say something to them: to apologize, to explain. But she sees from their stony faces that they do not care how she feels at all.

She runs down the hall in tears. She had never

worried about Robert, she always knew he would arrive home safely, that he would return to her. She, who in bad lonely times in her life, built an arsenal of totems—lighting candles in foreign churches, wearing her children's clothes—had never for a second doubted Robert's ability to conquer, to survive. Now, she sees, of course, that she was wrong about assuming anything; she will not take that risk again.

13

He cannot leave his wife. In the end, it is that simple. When did he begin knowing this? she asks him in barely a whisper. It has always been this way.

He cannot hear across the grotesque movable bed and has to ask her to crank it up so he is closer to her.

"When did you start feeling like this?" The words stick in her throat. "Was Louise here?"

"Yes." He lifts himself clumsily, reaches out a hand to her. "Baby, come here. " She rushes to his side, kneels by the bed, lays her head on the cool sheets, starts to weep.

"Oh, little love, don't. Oh, my little love." His chest hurts. He stops and gulps, takes some shallow breaths.

She sees this and tenses, and for one minute, she thinks she will let him die, she will kill him the way he is killing her.

She walks through the hospital alone. It is late

at night. All around her is death and she thinks of death. It is as if their love affair was a child to whom they gave life, but it was born too late, too small and could only survive a short time and now is dead. She knows she will mourn it the rest of her life. She knows he will remember it with pain, but as the years pass, the pain will fade to pleasure and fondness. She will mourn it as one mourns a dead child.

She remembers looking out the bedroom window one night last July, when fireflies had lighted up the lower branches of the trees so they looked on fire and thinking, my life will never be better than this moment. Or a day in August, sitting out on the river and Robert felt a breeze that was cool, unusual. "Did you feel that, love?" he asked. "What?" She was lying back, her bare feet on the railing of a fence, her face tilted up to the sun. "Sometime in late July or early August, there is a dip, a drop and the back of summer is broken. It gets hot again, but just for a little while, not the way it was before. After that, it will never be the same again."

Now she will become old quickly, her hair will fade, begin to gray; she will assume the odd androgyny that comes with age. She will stop bothering with estrogen supplements, with hair color and nail polish, her legs will go unshaven. She will thicken, not get really fat, but her waist will thicken and her thighs will spread and there will be no reason to exercise. Whiskers will grow in her chin and she will forget to tweeze them. She will work very hard and write many books. She will wear sensible shoes and get a very small barky dog. Robert will be dead within a year.

But it doesn't happen that way. Things conspire to return her to life. Monique asks her to assume the editorship of the journal so she can have a leave at the University in Berlin next year. Five boxes of manuscripts and files appear magically—FedEx—at the end of the week. She cleans off the little desk in the music room where Lucia slept at her feet and plugs in her computer. In a wooden wine crate she finds the manuscript of the book on housewives, reads it with a certain pleasure and begins to mark things in the margin.

She gets a phone call from a woman at the local high school. They have received some state arts money and wonders if she'd give a course for their adult education series beginning in February: art history, or painting, or women, anything the woman says, they are so happy she is here, they just found out. They can't pay much, the woman adds cautiously. But it is enough to buy a puppy from the litter whose photo of yellow lab puppies, stuffed like white peaches into a basket, appeared on the bulletin board at the store a few weeks ago.

Amy and Josh and his new girl friend are coming next week for Christmas and Suzanne is forced into the apple barn for sheets and comforters. She hangs them out on the split rail fences in the frigid air; they smell better than they ever did. She washes the sheets in bleach and finds recipes for cookies she hasn't made in years: Swedish ginger snaps, almond crescents of Oma's, pecans sautéed in butter and cinnamon and sugar.

Then she thinks she will make black-eyed peas for New Year's Day and she will call Robert for the recipe. He can hardly refuse such a small request. She rushes into the house, drops the recipe folder onto the table and, hands trembling, dials his private number at work. She knows he is back at work because she allowed herself to call once, before, but again, when she hears his voice—steady, strong, true— she cannot speak and hangs up. She is sure he knows who it is.

Suddenly, she is filled with longing for him, the kind of longing that defined the winter of their romance, after she realized she loved him and they were separated by hours and days, and even after he moved out to the country with her and everything—his wife, his daughters, the distance, his work, his guilt—conspired to keep them apart. She looks around their little house and sees how they had begun to make a life with the swatches and pieces of different pasts. He has left some of his things and from certain angles he is still there.

Now he is a traveler but she remains. Now, in the middle of the night, she cannot sleep. She leaves the bed where she slept next to the man she loved for such a short time, but more than any man she had loved except her father and her son, who were not carnal loves, but loves of the spirit, the soul. This man she loved with everything. She goes downstairs into this cold, still strange house. It is quiet. The dog she loved is recently dead, at her command, although she had no choice. She is between dogs, between lives and she cannot sleep. She is restless. The fire has died and she does not bother to retrieve it. She pulls a notebook from the table behind, lies in the narrow love seat from his office, covers herself with a mohair shawl and begins to write in the book about changes. She remembers how, in the months before she left her home, her old life, she had frequently consulted the I Ching. She had thrown: The Family, Keeping Still, Inner Truth, Dispersion, Differently at the Beginning.

Last week a gift came; there was no card. It

was the telescope in a narrow wooden box that opened like a puzzle, the two uneven pieces joined invisibly. It was wrapped in a piece of chamois that was so dark blue, it was the color of night. The cloth was so worn it felt like velvet; the folds were like a thick batter around the old brass instrument. She took it out and held it to her eye and smoothed it with both her hands. It was cold and hard, with an amazing capacity to grow. She put it back in the box for next summer.

She imagines how they will meet. She imagines the day she will be downtown and she will see him crossing the street at Michigan and Wacker Drive. She will be wearing her purple hat with the trim of fox she bought years ago in Paris and he calls her Anna Karenina hat. Or maybe the black pleated scarf with jet beads she bought when she knew she was falling in love with him. Or they will be at the Art Institute in the rooms where the Impressionist paintings hang, the men in top hats with sharp waxed mustaches, the women with a single velvet strand tied around their bare white throats. She will tell him how Manet went to Madrid and saw the black in Valesquez and Goya.

She will be Scheherezade. She will tell him she recently read the story of a man who had always loved the sound of rain as a child, how it had brought great comfort in his orphaned childhood and how when he was dying, the woman who loved him, his lover, not his wife, turned a hose onto the tiled roof above his bedroom, so he could hear the sound again before he died.

I am with you, *Parigi*, do you feel my presence? she whispers when she walks along the river or sits alone at night by the fire he tended or drives the endless miles into the city to do what: to find him, of course.

When she finds him she will put her hand in his and will say, I am small and soft and smell of jasmine and roses, and I come with all my imperfections and my pettiness and my prejudices and my handful of stories, and I sit in your pocket with your pipe and I fit into your mouth and I fit into your hand. I smooth back your brow, I touch you softly on the tips of your shoulders and I call you love.

She will find him.

The Author

Annette Williams Jaffee is the author of two novels, *Adult Education* (Ontario Review) and *Recent History* (Putnam). She lives on the Delaware River in Bucks County, Pennsylvania.

This first English language edition of *The Dangerous Age* was printed for The Leapfrog Press in 1998 by Cushing–Malloy. Typeface is Monotype Bembo, a 1929 design supervised by Stanley Morison and based on typefaces cut by Francesco Griffo in 1495. Composed and set by John Taylor-Convery at JTC Imagineering.